C000179683

# OLIVER VII

ANTAL SZERB

# OLIVER VII

Translated from the Hungarian by
Len Rix

PUSHKIN PRESS
LONDON

*Duty is not a bed of roses*
Montanhagol

English translation © Len Rix 2007

First published in Hungarian as
*Oliver VII* in 1942
© Estate of Antal Szerb

This edition first published in 2007 by

Pushkin Press
12 Chester Terrace
London NW1 4ND

ISBN (13) 978 1 901285 79 6
ISBN (10) 1 901285 79 0

Cover: *Our Big Men* 1927 László Moholy-Nagy
© Collection Hattula Moholy-Nagy/DACS London 2007

Frontispiece: Antal Szerb

Set in 10 on 12 Baskerville
and printed in Great Britain by TJ International Ltd
Padstow Cornwall

# OLIVER VII

S ANDOVAL THE PAINTER had tactfully left the young couple to themselves—the word 'young' being used here in a rather specialised sense. The dancer certainly was young. Officially seventeen, she could not in truth have been much older. Count Antas, however, was more like sixty, at the very least.

The Chateau Madrid coffee house, on whose terrace they were sitting, was the supremely fashionable place in which to be seen in early spring, with its pavilion under the celebrated hundred-year-old plane trees beside the little lake in the park that began where the city ended. Given the small number of these open-air coffee houses in the state of Alturia during those years before the war, you might have expected to have to fight for a seat. However, at the Chateau Madrid the breeze was included in the bill. With a cup of coffee costing three Alturian taller, the clientele consisted solely of the social elite and the *demi-monde*. On this particular day, with the steadily worsening financial crisis, it was less than full.

In front of the Count rose a tall stack of side plates, one for every drink he had imbibed. The Count drank himself into a stupor most evenings, but, not being a man of narrow principles, he had no objection to drinking in the afternoon as well. In fact, he had probably been at it that morning too—it was hard to say quite when he had begun: normally he would have known better than to appear before so large a gathering in the company of a little dancing girl of such

9

dubious reputation. (In those years before the war women still had such things.) Luckily the trellised bower they were in offered a shield from prying eyes.

"My gazelle!" he murmured amorously. The little dancer acknowledged this compliment with a guarded smile.

"My antelope!" he continued, developing his theme. He sensed the need for yet another animal, but could think of nothing better than a pelican.

At that precise moment Sandoval burst in, with an anxious face.

"Your Excellency! … "

"My boy," the Count began, in a voice that verged on a hiss. He did not welcome intrusion. But Sandoval cut him short.

"Count," he insisted, "Her Ladyship is here, with her companion."

Antas clapped the monocle to his eye and stared around. It was beyond question. Slowly, terrifyingly, like a fully rigged old-style frigate, his wife was negotiating the entrance.

"I'm done for!" he stammered, his eyes darting hither and thither, as if some unexpected source of assistance might come sailing through the air.

"We can still get away," whispered Sandoval. "We can nip out through the kitchen and straight into the car. Come on, Count, be quick … and try to look like someone completely different."

"And the bill?" demanded the grandee, a gentleman through and through.

Sandoval tossed a fifty taller note onto the table.

"We must go. Quickly!"

They dashed out of the bower, Antas with averted face. Almost immediately he collided with a waiter balancing a tray in his hand. The crash of broken crockery brought all eyes to bear upon them. Antas began to apologise, but Sandoval seized him and led him, at a speed scarcely to be credited, through the kitchen, out onto the street and into the car, losing the girl somewhere along the way.

"You don't think she saw me?" the Count asked, slamming the door shut behind them.

"I'm afraid it's quite certain she did. When Your Excellency knocked the waiter over everyone—including the Countess—turned to look. So far as I could make out, in my state of agitation, she was shaking her parasol at you."

Antas slumped back into the seat.

"That's it. I'm dead," he whimpered.

Sandoval meanwhile had started the engine and swerved out onto the main road leading to the city. There had been no time to send for the driver, and they left him to his fate.

"If I might make a suggestion … " said Sandoval, breaking the horrified silence.

"I'm listening," the Count whispered, in the tones of a man whose life was about to expire.

"The fact that Your Excellency met Her Ladyship is not something we can do anything about. But time is always a great healer."

"What do you mean?"

"For example, if Your Excellency were to disappear for a few days—a week, shall we say? During that time her rage would subside, and she would start to worry, not being able to imagine where you might be … and it would give me time to think up some story or other to put a plausible front on what happened … "

"How could I disappear, my boy? Me, the Royal Chief Steward? How could you think that? Such a prominent public figure!"

"True, true. Just let me think for a moment … I have it! I'll take Your Excellency to the country mansion of a friend of mine, up in the Lidarini Mountains. It's utterly remote. The post takes a week to get there. Trenmor, my friend, is abroad at the moment, but the staff know me well—they'll obey me without question—and you'll be completely safe up there, where no bird flies. Even if you wanted to, you wouldn't be able to leave until I came for you with the car."

"Good, good, my boy. Take me wherever you wish. Just don't let me see my wife, and above all, don't let her see me! And make sure you never get married."

The car turned round and set off in the opposite direction, away from the city. Soon the Count was fast asleep. He woke again only when they reached the mansion. There Sandoval handed him over to the household staff and took his leave, promising to return once the skies over the marital home had cleared. Antas thanked him profusely for his services, and Sandoval hurried back to the capital.

12

It was late evening when he arrived in Lara. There were far fewer people than usual on the streets, but he noticed a lot of soldiers. The storm that had overtaken his car on the road had now died down, but dark clouds continued to race across the sky.

"It's the same up there," he thought, studying them with his painter's eye. "The sky is as restless as I am. Well, not many artists get the chance to play a role in major historical events. Perhaps only Rubens … "

The car squealed to a halt outside a large, unlit building and he leapt out. *The Barrel-makers Joint Stock Trading Company*, proclaimed a rather tasteless sign.

"Even the notices in this country need a revolution," he muttered to himself.

He applied his weight to a bell.

A narrow section of the vast door opened, and someone peered out cautiously.

"*The barrels from Docasillades*," he announced, with significant emphasis.

"*Come in—we're checking the staves*," a voice replied, and Sandoval entered.

"Good evening, Partan," he said to the doorman, who was wearing a leather coat and bandolier. "*The eighteenth?*"

"*Upstairs in the balancing room.*"

He made his way rapidly up the poorly lit stairwell and arrived at a door. In gold lettering on a black plaque he read the word 'Accounts'. Inside, a group of about ten men were sitting on benches around the walls. They were oddly dressed, with the sort of intense faces you see

13

only in times of historic upheaval. "Who are they? And what might they be in civilian life?" he wondered. The majority had strange bulges in their clothing, caused by ill-concealed pistols. They seemed to know who he was and simply stared at him without interest. A young man got up from a table at the far end of the room and came rapidly over to him.

"Well, at least you got here, Sandoval. We've been waiting a long time. Come this way."

Sandoval followed him into the next room.

It was small and almost completely empty apart from an oddly shaped telephone—one of the stages along the secret line. Beside it sat two men, smoking.

The first, with his black suit, gold-rimmed spectacles and impossibly narrow face, was Dr Delorme. Sandoval knew him well, and went across to him. The other man he had never seen before. He was extremely tall, with an austere, intelligent face; his hair, which was unusually straight for an Alturian, was slicked down flat against his head.

"Sandoval," Delorme introduced him to the stranger.

The man clicked his heels, held out his hand, but did not give his name. Then he drew back into a dimly lit corner of the room.

"Well?" asked Delorme.

"I spent fifty taller," Sandoval replied. "I paid the bill at the Chateau Madrid."

It amused him to see how much it disconcerted Delorme that he should begin with this trivial demand. Delorme was obviously struggling to conceal his nervous excitement.

"Of course. Here you are." He handed over a fifty taller note.

"And now, if you would be so kind as to give us your report."

"No," thought Sandoval, "you could never make him forget his manners. He's not what you'd imagine, for a rabid demagogue."

And he recounted his tale. As he spoke, the stranger drew closer to him, studying him intently.

"Splendid, really splendid!" remarked Delorme. "Only an artist could have accomplished that. I particularly like the way you timed the Countess' arrival."

"It was very simple. I sent her an anonymous letter saying that if she wished to expose her husband she should come to the Chateau Madrid at six. I know how jealous she is."

Delorme turned to the stranger.

"This place in the country where they've taken him is manned by our people, masquerading as household staff. If necessary, they'll detain him by force. But it won't be needed. Fear of his wife will be much more effective."

"Thank you, Sandoval," said the stranger, and again offered his hand.

"Glad to be of service. Might I ask one favour in return? I don't like being a blind instrument. If there's no special reason why you can't, would you explain why it was necessary to get that pious idiot out of the capital?"

"Why?" the stranger replied. "Because it's his job as

Chief Steward to select the regiment responsible for guarding the palace the following day. Since he won't be there tomorrow, I shall have to choose it myself."

Sandoval glanced quizzically at Delorme.

"The gentleman you are speaking with is Major Mawiras-Tendal, His Highness' principal *aide-de-camp*."

Sandoval bowed, rather maladroitly. What he had heard astonished him. The King's *aide-de-camp* and close friend was involved in this business? How very widespread the discontent must be …

It had barely touched him personally. As a mere painter he understood little of the economic problems that had produced it. The King himself was a kind and intelligent man, extremely sympathetic in Sandoval's opinion. It was only his loathing of petty-bourgeois complacency that had brought him into Delorme's camp. That, and the love of gambling, and of the unexpected—in a word, the desire to live dangerously.

"And the day after tomorrow," the Major continued, "the Twelfth Regiment is on guard at the palace. It's the one regiment in which we can count on every man. Do you follow me?"

"So, then. The day after tomorrow?"

"The day after tomorrow."

The Major shook hands and left. Sandoval stood staring after him, speechless.

"Well, well. He too?"

"He especially. He's closer than anyone to the Nameless Captain."

"Extraordinary."

16

"Don't forget that Mawiras-Tendal is the grandson of the great revolutionary hero after whom every street in Alturia is named."

"Blood being thicker than water … "

"So it seems. Sometimes these truisms turn out to be true. Life holds no greater surprise."

"Have you any orders for me, for tomorrow?"

"My orders? I must ask just one thing of you. I'd be very glad if you would take yourself off to Algarthe and call on the Duke. You're the only one of our people they'll allow in, now that he's kept under such close guard. They know you as his portrait painter, and the thing is, no one will take you seriously. That's why you are so priceless to us."

"I must resist this notion of pricelessness. I can be paid at any time … "

"I know," Delorme replied with a smile. "And I am sure you've had little cause to complain so far. I was thinking of pricelessness in the moral sense. So, then, Algarthe … "—and he stroked his forehead wearily. He seemed to be having difficulty focusing his thoughts. Then he continued:

"My God, I'm so tired. After we've brought this revolution off I shall retire for a fortnight to that sanatorium for journalists. If only I don't have to become Prime Minister! Anyway, as I said, Algarthe … have a word with the Duke. You know how to talk to him. Try to knock some sense into him. Prepare him for what's coming. If it comes completely out of the blue, he's so frail it could affect him badly. It could even kill him, and then we're right back where we started. Send me a report on his condition afterwards. And now, God go with you. I've got a whole series of reports to get through tonight. About the navy, the universities, the winegrowers' association, the market traders ... we're carrying the whole country on our backs. God be with you. And please, spare me the password, and can we do without with the secret handshake? I'm tired."

The situation in Alturia was as follows. Simon II, father of the present king, Oliver VII, had been an outstanding ruler, and the country had suffered in consequence ever since. He modernised the army uniform, established elementary schools, introduced telephones, public ablutions and much else besides, and all this benevolent activity had exhausted the state finances. Besides, as we all know from our geography books, the Alturian people are of a somewhat dreamy nature, fanciful and poetically inclined.

Along with the throne, Oliver inherited a chaotic financial situation. A man of true Alturian blood, he shared the dreamy nature of his people and showed little aptitude for fiscal matters. It seems too that he was unfortunate in his choice of advisers, who grew steadily richer as the public purse grew lean. To pay the state representatives on the first of each month the Finance Minister had at times to resort to near-farcical expedients, such as doling out their entire salaries and expenses in copper coins from the toll on the capital's Chain Bridge. Malicious tongues even claimed that it was his masked men who carried out that daring break-in at the Lara branch of Barclays Bank.

At that point the Finance Minister, Pritanez, in an attempt to head off the discontent that was reaching revolutionary fervour, accepted a plan to reorganise the entire economy.

The Alturian people's almost exclusive sources of revenue were wine and the sardine—the famous red wine of Alturia, preserving in drinkable form the memory of southern days and southern summers; and the famous Alturian sardine, a small but congenial creature, the comfort of travellers and elderly bachelors alike, when served in oil, or with a little fresh tomato. For centuries the principal market for Alturian wine and sardines had been the affluent citizens of Norlandia, under whose gloomy skies the grape never grew, and whose chilly shores the sardine took care to avoid.

When, in the early years of Oliver's reign, the national purse began to show alarming signs of atrophy, Finance Minister Pritanez received a visit one fine day from the renowned Coltor. This Coltor was the greatest business tycoon in Norlandia. Legends abounded of his unbelievable wealth, and of his astonishing talent for buying and selling. He did not deal in mines, factories, land or newspapers, as did other great financiers. Instead he marketed innovations. For example, throughout Norlandia and all the neighbouring states, he retailed a half-pair of shoes, to be purchased in case of inadvertent loss of the other half. By some remarkable feat of technical ingenuity the left shoe would also fit the right foot and the right shoe the left. It was he who introduced the practice of building house walls with onions, developed the textile cigarette and the ant-powered spirit lamp; and he who found a way to convert the famous fogs of his homeland into edible oil. There was no counting the number of discoveries he had harnessed for economic exploitation.

And then, after all that buying and selling, it occurred to him that you could also buy a country. The proposal made to Pritanez was that he, Coltor, would take control of the entire wine and sardine production of Alturia. In return he would put the nation's chaotic finances in order. The Alturians were poetical souls, for whom the whole tedious business of money was just a source of worry and disappointment, but now he was offering to lift this burden from the nation's shoulders.

Pritanez embraced this proposal with the greatest enthusiasm, not least because the contract, once signed, offered him personal prospects such as the finance minister of an impecunious little country could only dream of—presuming, of course, that he addressed the issue with the resolution of a Cesare Borgia. Determination was not one of his characteristics. He was a rotund, circumspect individual, who lived in a perpetual state of terror.

By extending similar blandishments to his fellow ministers, Pritanez managed to secure their support. But that still left the most important item of all, the consent of the King. From the outset, Oliver had opposed the plan with unusual vigour. He would not hear of his country being sold to foreigners, and he turned a bright red if Pritanez ever dared mention it. The man was beginning to sense that the whole wonderful scheme would come to nothing, because of the stupid pig-headedness of a callow youth.

Coltor meanwhile went on developing the plan in ever finer detail, as if no obstacle to it could possibly arise from the Alturian side. He managed to rouse interest in it even in those ruling circles in his own country that had initially thought it rather ambitious, and their enthusiasm had grown steadily. In the end, the Norlandian government had adopted the scheme as its own, and Baron Birker, their ambassador in Lara, had done his best to win the King over. Eventually, it seemed, Birker's reasoning had prevailed: Oliver now saw that his country had no other means of escape from financial chaos, and he finally accepted that he would have to put his name to the document.

Even so, the Norlandian government still felt it necessary to make sure that the King did not change his mind with the passing of time, and that he would continue to believe in the plan and support it. The best way to ensure that, it seemed to them, as a nation deeply committed to family life, would be to bind the King to their own ruling house by personal ties. They proposed that Oliver should take Princess Ortrud, daughter of the Emperor of Norlandia, as his wife.

Oliver had not the slightest objection to this idea. He had known Ortrud since childhood, when they had played together in the dust of the Imperial Palace gardens. She was a handsome, cultivated young woman, and they had always been the very best of friends.

However, when the news was given to the citizens of Alturia that they would soon acquire a queen in the person of Ortrud, a difficulty began to emerge. Normally they were as enthusiastic about such royal goings-on as the citizens of any other country, and their government had counted on this feeling. But it did not materialise. The press made great play of the fact that never before in the history of their Catholic nation had the king married a Protestant. One way and another, all sorts of absurd rumours began to circulate, most notably that the male members of the Norlandian royal family had been, for over a hundred years and without a single exception, drunkards, philanderers or half-wits. Some of the dailies went so far as to issue lurid pamphlets alleging that Emperor Eustace IV had stolen one of the smaller state crowns as a pledge for a Greek pawnbroker, and that Prince Simiskes had drowned in a barrel of rainwater when inebriated.

Then one day the real scandal broke.

The opposition press got wind of the Coltor Plan and announced the news with the full panoply of suitably outraged comment. What was particularly strange about all this was that only the King and his ministers— none of whom had anything to gain from a premature disclosure—had been party to the information. From that point onwards they viewed each other with even greater distrust, double-checking their wallets as they went into cabinet meetings, and burning their account books before leaving home. But for all their vigilance, they never discovered who the traitor was.

This marked the start of the role played by the fire-eating Dr Delorme. Here was a treasonous plan, which would bring total destruction on the state of Alturia! Day after day his ranting editorials poured out molten lava against it—it was scarcely credible that one man could carry so much lava inside himself. And these daily outpourings were devoured with ever greater eagerness by the population. The government made one or two clumsy attempts to silence the press, but in that archaic world the techniques for doing so were still remarkably undeveloped.

The young King became more and more personally unpopular. Prior to this, the good-hearted Alturian people had always taken a misty-eyed delight in his youthfulness. Now, when he appeared in public, he was met by sullen, hostile looks. His oleograph portraits were stripped from the walls of public houses, and the popular baby soap, cider and travelling basket that carried his image became unsellable, however great the discount offered by their horrified vendors. The Alturian people, like southern races everywhere, loved to express their political opinions in the form of slogans daubed on walls. Now, instead of the universal *Long live the King!* and *Oliver our pride and joy!* there was a steady shift to such sentiments as: *Foreigners out!*, *Death to Coltor!* and *Keep our sardines free!*

The unrest was quietly fomented by underground organisations. The Alturians, although gentle and dreamy by nature, were born conspirators. For decades they had channelled all their sporting inclinations in this direction, and the plotters, as we noted earlier, came from every level of society. Following ancient tradition, they swore an oath of loyalty to the 'Nameless Captain'. There were those who thought that this being was a mere mythical notion, but others, the majority, were convinced he was a real person, who would come forward and declare himself at the critical moment.

The conspirators' stated aim was to force the abdication of Oliver VII and replace him with the country's grand old man, Geront, Duke of Algarthe—the person on whom Sandoval was to call the following day.

The one-hour taxi ride from Lara to Algarthe was not cheap, but that too was added to Sandoval's expense account with the Revolutionary Committee. A man on a mission for important conspirators can hardly take the suburban train.

Some ten minutes before they reached the mansion, the car was stopped.

"Excuse me, sir—customs check," said the military officer, whose appearance was so aristocratic Sandoval found it hard to believe that this was a matter of routine customs harassment. There was no inspection process, only questions about his name and the purpose of his journey. When he explained who he was, and that he was painting the Duke's portrait, the officer saluted politely and waved him on.

The taxi turned into the park and proceeded up the broad yellow driveway. Two astonishingly ancient footmen stepped forward, opened the door and greeted him affably.

"His Highness will be delighted to see you," they assured him. "So few people have come this way recently … "

Sandoval made his way through the foyer, whose walls were hung with vast historic canvasses in the somewhat rhetorical style of the mid-nineteenth century. The Duke's taste was for delicate miniatures, and these hereditary daubings had been banished to the entrance. In the second room stood some small earthenware statues; in the third, cupboards filled with *kamea*—little square objects engraved with kabbalistic symbols; in the fourth the Duke's renowned collection of keys. Everything was in exemplary order.

He moved quickly on, up the inner stairway, to the Duke's private apartments. In a room packed with Japanese watercolours another praeternaturally ancient footman received him and offered him a chair.

In no time at all Duke Geront appeared, supported by a young woman. The claimant to the throne was seventy-five years old and in rather poor condition for his years. He wore extremely thick spectacles, groping his way ahead as he walked, and his voice wavered into a sort of bleat; but his manner was decisive and intelligent. There was much more life in the girl, Princess Clodia. She was about thirty years of age, energetic and rather stern of feature: handsome enough, but as an old

25

woman, Sandoval thought to himself, she would be really formidable.

"Ah, Sandoval," the Princess cried, "so they let you through the cordon? How did you manage it? They have practically sealed us off from the outside world. Our mail is opened, they listen in on our telephone calls … "

"You must remember, your Highness, that you are a claimant to the throne. There is a price to pay for that."

"Have you brought news from the Committee?"

"Yes. Here, in my pocket."

He handed over a thick envelope.

"Thank you, Sandoval. I'll go and read it up in my room. Meanwhile you may entertain my father."

After a long search the Duke produced a *netsuke* from his pocket—a little button carved from stone and used for clasping the kimono at the shoulder.

"Marvellous," he commented. "Fifteenth century."

They talked at length about the netsuke and other things Japanese, the Duke leading him with uncertain steps through room after room, bringing out his treasures to show them off. Sandoval made tactful but persistent attempts to introduce the subject of what was to happen the following day, but even the most oblique mention of any such topic produced a display of violent irritation.

"All these stupid claims to the throne," he muttered. "Don't say one word about any of that. Nothing will come of it, I'm quite sure. In my late brother Simon's reign I was next in line three times … or was it just twice? … and nothing ever came of it. All the better for it, too."

A full half-hour or more passed in this manner, before signs of fatigue began to show on the Duke's face. Princess Clodia and a footman came for him soon after, and made him lie down on a divan.

Clodia and Sandoval went through into another room.

"He's interested in nothing but his collections," she complained. "But he always was like that. He's spent his entire fortune on them, and he's run up so many debts he won't be able to pay them even if he does become king. Oh well, never mind. It's lucky I'm here. It's not that I have an especially high opinion of myself, but I could run this country every bit as well as that daft cousin of mine, Oliver. Even when we were children he was completely useless. He used to write poetry … "

"Your Highness, the people are always happy to be ruled over by a woman. Because the male monarchs are always swayed by their women, and the women by their men."

For a moment the Princess frowned at this extreme impertinence, then she smiled. She thought of those exemplary women whose lives she had studied with such care: Elizabeth of England, Catherine the Great … Yes, Sandoval was right.

"The Duke will have to be shaken out of his apathy," Sandoval continued. "Tomorrow is the day we've all been waiting for. For a little while at least, he ought to show some enthusiasm and appetite for the job in hand. By this time the day after tomorrow, assuming all goes well, he'll be king—and he still won't let us mention it in his presence."

"You are quite right. His lack of interest could be very damaging when he comes face to face with his supporters. It might even turn the Nameless Captain against him."

"The Nameless Captain? Does Your Highness believe in such a being?"

"Of course. I don't understand how you could think otherwise. Who do you imagine is funding the revolution? You don't think it's us, in Algarthe? We haven't a penny to our name … "

"True, true. But then who could this Nameless Captain be? Who in Alturia has that sort of money? And is it possible that Your Highness really doesn't know?"

"Well, that's how it is: even I don't know. I have speculated about various foreign powers and interests, but none of them seems very probable. I simply cannot imagine who would have anything to gain from my father's taking the throne."

"Delorme insists that the Nameless Captain will declare himself at the critical moment. Perhaps we'll see him tomorrow. Meanwhile I must speak to the Duke and have one last try. Does Your Highness think he might be fully rested by now?"

"Yes, I should think so. Shall we go and see?"

The Duke was completely his old self again. He greeted Sandoval with delight, having forgotten that he had met him earlier.

"What news, Sandoval? Would you like to see something really special?" And he produced the netsuke again. "Marvellous, eh? Fifteenth century."

28

Sandoval expressed proper admiration for the carving, then said:

"And I've brought you something rather fine."

"What's that? One of your own paintings?" the Duke began, rather anxiously, as Sandoval produced a lengthy scroll.

"No, no. Here you are. How do you like this etching?"

The Duke peered at it, initially rather unsure, then his face lit up, and he immersed himself with increasing delight in contemplation of the picture.

"But it's a Piranesi! Why didn't you say so at the start? It's wonderful! From his best period! How in the devil's name did you come by this? If it's for sale I'll buy it immediately."

"But Father … !" Princess Clodia broke in, clearly exasperated. "You know how … And you, Sandoval, why are you teasing him like this?"

"It's not for sale," Sandoval hastened to reassure her. "It belongs to the National Gallery in Lara—the Director is a close friend. He lent it to me, on the side."

"Would you let me have it on loan, then? Or as a present?" the Duke began. And his face filled with a child-like yearning. "I've always longed for a Piranesi like this. Only this sort, mind you; none of the others."

"I'm sorry, but the Director has no power to give the gallery's treasures away. That would require an order from the highest level."

"The devil with all that. You know perfectly well that I give orders to no one in this country. Take your picture away. Take it away!"

Petulantly, he turned his face to the wall.

"But Your Highness, the day after tomorrow … "

"What about the day after tomorrow? Are you insane?"

"Your Highness, you must remember that, very soon, you will be the highest authority in the land, and it will be yours to command."

"Yes, I know. I've heard that so often. And as soon as I wanted to buy that tiny little Ostade, all hell broke loose … "

"But when Your Highness is King of Alturia, it will be an entirely different matter."

"What do you mean? You know Alturia. Do you think kings here have money for paintings? All they can afford is their own portraits. Or … will I really be able to have them for nothing?"

"Your Highness simply instructs the Minister of Culture that such and such a picture is to be transferred from the National Gallery to the Royal Palace, or, if you like, here to Algarthe."

"Is that right? Can I really do that? I'd never thought of that."

He pondered the idea.

"That changes everything," he said, after a pause. His voice was fresh, almost youthful. "That makes the whole thing much more interesting. Why didn't you say so at the start? So, where are these revolutionaries? Let's see them; let's have a look at them. I want action, not empty words! Clodia, I hope you've made all the necessary arrangements. I'll keep the Piranesi here anyway."

He plucked the picture out of Sandoval's hands and disappeared with astonishing speed into the next room.

"That was an excellent idea," said Clodia. "Let's hope he hasn't forgotten it by the morning."

"Your Highness, I shall leave you the National Gallery catalogue. Please study it carefully. If the Duke seems to be losing interest, just repeat one or two little propositions: Fouquet … Boltraffio. And a genuine Van Eyck."

He left the mansion soon after. Once inside the taxi, he sank into a pleasant daydream.

The calendar pursued its relentless course, and the next day was indeed the eighth of April. In the morning Sandoval reported to the revolutionary committee in the Barrel- Makers Joint Stock Trading Company building, and learnt that the whole plan was moving punctually towards its goal. On early morning trains, on foot, in hay-wagons and specially hired coaches, a mighty throng of aggrieved fishermen and winegrowers had arrived in the capital and been lodged in garages, cellars and attics, to keep them out-of-sight until the moment of action arrived. Meanwhile the Twelfth Regiment was on duty at the palace.

Even the streets had taken on an unusual appearance. The presence of flags flying to mark the next day's royal wedding lent them a festive air. Everywhere banners, garlands of flowers and other insignia lauded King Oliver VII and his bride-to-be, Princess Ortrud.

Sandoval was visited by the strange, oddly perverse feeling that this carnival atmosphere, created ostensibly to honour the King, would in fact prepare the way for his dethronement. Inside the great Westros department store he noted the huge portraits, seemingly made from entire rolls of silk and broadcloth, of the King and Princess, and he shuddered to think of the ironic workings of destiny. A great many shops and businesses were closed—officially for the approaching celebration, but actually because the owners feared for the safety of their windows and warehouses in the events that were about to unfold.

On the afternoon of that memorable day a ministerial council of the highest importance was taking place in the royal palace. The moment had arrived for the signing of Finance Minister Pritanez's great work, the Coltor Treaty.

They had been in session for quite some time, deliberating every detail before the arrival of the King. The Minister for Internal Affairs was concerned about reports he was receiving of serious unrest across the country. The Prime Minister remained optimistic:

"Nonsense; this is Alturia, remember. Our people are always hatching plots and conspiracies, and in the end everything stays exactly as it was. Think of the time when Balázs II or the Unfortunate was strung up by the heels. They took him down five minutes later, and he continued to rule to general acclaim."

At that moment King Oliver entered the chamber, accompanied by his *aide-de-camp*, Major Mawiras-Tendal. The King, who is in fact the hero of our history, is a young man of twenty-four, with a handsome, rather dreamy face, one that might seem perfectly at home on an athletics track or in a nightclub, or, come to that, since its finely formed brow betrays an unusual intelligence, in the comfortable room of a library hung with portraits. Here, among the stern and generally rather misshapen features of his fellow countrymen, he seems somehow out-of-place. The incongruity of his appearance is intensified by the uniform he is wearing. It is a field marshal's greatcoat, magnificent, severe and severely old-fashioned, with high-winged collars. It visibly restricts his every movement, and weighs no less heavily on his mind. He is forever complaining about having to wear it: "I can't get comfortable in it," he insists. "It's like sitting on a cactus, or as if I'd become a cactus myself." But tradition decrees that he can never take it off. The kings of Alturia have gone about in full field marshal regalia ever since one of their ancestors, Philip II or the One-Eared, suffered the indignity of having his enemies burst in upon him while he was wandering down a palace corridor in his nightshirt.

The King greeted each of his ministers in turn, then withdrew with his Prime Minister and Minister of the Interior for a private discussion.

"Your Highness," the Prime Minister began, "this is a rather delicate matter, and a rather bold step to take, but we believe that Your Highness' *aide-de-camp*, Major Mawiras-Tendal, is not a suitable person to be carrying out a duty of trust beside Your Highness in critical moments like these."

"Mawiras-Tendal not suitable? What possible objection can there be to him? He's a first-class soldier, and an even better friend."

"Your Highness," the Interior Minister interposed, "I'm afraid that—from confidential reports—we are only too well informed of the Major's political views. He is in contact with the leaders of the opposition press, and, worse, with the fire-eating Delorme himself. He is in regular correspondence with political exiles abroad. Besides all this, he is the grandson of our national hero, whose sole bequest to us as a people was a predisposition to anarchy.

"This would be a highly suitable moment to get rid of him," the minister continued. "The post has become vacant of Director of the State Mercury Mines. Poor Colowar died the day before yesterday, of poisoning."

"Mercury poisoning?" the horrified King asked.

"No, alcohol poisoning. Mawiras-Tendal would be just the person to replace him."

"My dear sirs, we cannot possibly discuss this now. How could you think it? You surely know that I would part with anyone rather than my old Milán. He's the best person for the job, and my most sincere friend. But if you wish, we can talk about it tomorrow, or the day after."

"Why only then?" asked the Prime Minister, dumb-founded.

"Because by then so much will have changed. I shall be a married man. But meanwhile we have a duty to perform. Could we please get it over and done with? Let's swallow the bitter pill, and put our names to this famous treaty."

34

Everyone took his appointed place round a large circular table. The Finance Minister once again summarised the significance of the document while the others sat in a bored, restless silence waiting for the decisive moment of signing. Their restlessness stemmed from a shared feeling that the King's good breeding and seeming impartiality might well conceal some inscrutable, deeply impractical character—some unsuspected trait lurking beneath his general good sense. That he might, at the very last minute, change his mind.

But that did not happen.

Having listened carefully to all they had to say, he asked, in the most natural voice in the world:

"So, you gentlemen are all agreed that the country has no other means of salvation than for us to ratify this loathsome, humiliating treaty?"

"That is so," the Prime Minister answered. "If Your Highness does not sign it, and we fail to secure Coltor's advance payment, we might as well close down the Treasury and lock up the Chancellor. That is the stark reality."

"And you gentlemen are prepared to share with me the odium that will attach to this, that you … to put it politely … ? Well, you know what I am thinking."

"We shall stand by Your Highness to the last drop of our blood," the Prime Minister averred.

"We will give our all," the Minister for the Interior chimed in, "to the last drop of wine and the very last sardine."

"I do not doubt it. Then I can hesitate no longer. I shall

go down in history as the king for whom no sacrifice was too great. Kindly pass the document so that I may sign."

They watched, each man mouthing a prayer, as the King, very slowly, inscribed his name, and then stood for another moment, gazing in wonder at what he had written.

"So, all we need now is for you gentlemen to put your names to this document, and to send it on to the other signatory. With this I call the Royal Council to a close, and take my leave. Before it gets dark I would like to test-drive my new car, which arrived from Paris yesterday. And so, goodbye."

"Your Highness … " the Prime Minister began hesitantly.

"Well?"

"If you would grant another respectful request from your concerned well-wishers. Your Highness must surely be aware that the population is waiting in a fever of excitement for the signing of the treaty. Sadly, the opposition press has inflamed their feelings. It would seem advisable, in the interests of Your Highness' personal safety and of public order, that Your Highness should not leave the palace for one moment. At least, not before the wedding. The people will be calmer after that delightful ceremony."

The King hammered angrily on the table.

"This is outrageous. For two weeks now I have been under virtual house arrest. I can't go and play golf, because the road runs beside the military barracks. I can't go to the theatre, because the low light might favour an attempt on my life. I can't dine in the palace, because the head chef has republican sympathies. I can't go walking alone on Mt Lilión, or lie under an apple tree reading Dante. To say nothing of this damned coat … Who am I, to be debarred from every pleasure in life that any citizen of Alturia can enjoy? Everyone else can play golf and drive a car. Everyone, except me. So what am I then?"

The Prime Minister rose, bowed deeply, and declared:

"You are the King!"

The King's face darkened, and he muttered, very quietly: "Indeed."

"Your Highness well remembers," the Prime Minister continued, "those wonderful words of our great poet Montanhagol: 'duty is not a bed of roses'."

"Yes, of course. And on the subject of rose beds, I shall stay in tonight. But now I really must leave you gentlemen. My bride is waiting for me."

With much ceremonial bowing, the ministers departed. Pritanez set off at speed to the Palace Hotel, where Coltor's emissaries were waiting anxiously to know whether the King had signed or not. The favourable news was like a galvanic charge to their cold Norlandian blood. They shook Pritanez's hand warmly, and decided to celebrate the happy occasion with an expensive dinner later that evening. Then they talked over the final details of the down payment.

Pritanez left the hotel in a buoyant mood. His life's great work had come to a successful conclusion, and he would be a rich man. He was filled with an ecstatic sense of well-being. Everything in the world was wonderful: the ladies in horse-drawn carriages promenading under the palm trees in Montanhagol Avenue, the little coffee houses and their customers sitting outside on the pavements taking their ease, the clouds in the sky … for the first time in his life he noticed the clouds.

In that instant something utterly revolting smacked into his face. Something brown, moist, and excessively putrid. He recognised it from the smell: something horses were wont to leave behind them on the roads of that pre-war age.

Like thunder after lightning, this bull's-eye hit was followed by a loud yell; then a rotten egg came flying towards him, an onion, and sundry other objects. Confronted by the fact of his unpopularity, Pritanez ducked his head this way and that. But a crowd was advancing towards him with menacing gestures. He barely had time to leap into his car.

He was driven home, filled with disgust at his person and his clothing, which still retained the distinctive smell of each individual greeting in its ripe particularity. His house was a few steps away from the Palace Hotel.

But as they turned into the street where he lived, the chauffeur suddenly braked.

"Look, Your Excellency!"

An already substantial crowd was waiting outside the house, brandishing little flags and yelling. They too had no doubt equipped themselves with projectile materials. A chill went down Pritanez's spine.

The chauffeur did not wait for instructions. He reversed rapidly, and only after making his three-point turn did he ask where to go next.

"The Royal Palace," came the reply.

Gradually darkness fell. Huge crowds were milling around in the streets, faces never seen before in the capital. The plain-clothes security men had simply given up and melted into the throng.

In the general stir and bustle no one noticed the twenty conspirators making their way one-by-one towards the palace down various streets. There was a servants' door opening onto a neglected part of the park, used by delivery men during the day. This was where they broke into the building.

No force was actually needed. They knocked and gave the password of the day: The Ides of March. The door opened and a lieutenant of the Twelfth Regiment, armed to the teeth, admitted them one by one. It was not actually the fifteenth of March but the eighth. However, they rather liked the chilling reference to the great conspiracy that ended the life and sway of Julius Caesar.

A soldier led them down a series of dark corridors into the basement area, where they regrouped. An officer was waiting for them in a sort of hall, where he checked that all were present and immediately left.

Sandoval and Delorme were among them. Sandoval knew most of the others, either personally or by sight. They included a couple of rather wild, desperate characters— a newspaper delivery man famous for his strength, and an intensely evil-looking waiter. But the great majority seemed not too grimly aggressive, grim aggressiveness not featuring much in the Alturian character. Sandoval also noticed some of his more intellectual friends among them: a lawyer, a doctor and a writer.

A worrying thought suddenly struck him. It occurred to him that he had in fact received no instructions about what to do once they had broken into the palace. Delorme had said that they would work it out when they got there. At all events, Sandoval had brought his revolver.

"If this thing turns out badly," he thought, "I'll shoot myself. Or rather, I won't shoot myself. Who can say?"

Sandoval was a great raconteur. He had already given thought to the adventure he would narrate once he was free to talk about it at leisure amongst his fellow painters, around the club's dinner table at the Kina coffee house.

The door opened, and a respectful silence descended as the conspirators were joined by the imposing figure of Major Mawiras-Tendal.

"So, everyone's here. Follow me in absolute silence. No one must know you are in the building."

They made their way along a complicated and winding route through rooms and corridors, which the Major had carefully plotted to prevent them meeting a single soul—a feat made possible by the vast size of the palace, with its ancient, long-deserted wings and side-buildings.

Finally they arrived at the foot of a spiral staircase.

"Keep your wits about you," the Major said in a hushed voice: "This leads directly to the King's apartments."

They went up the creaking staircase, stopping and starting, and glaring recriminations at one another. One of them, a man with a permanently startled expression on his face and very little hair, turned suddenly to Sandoval:

"Zizigan. Cardboard box manufacturer," he announced, choosing his moment rather strangely.

"Torrer. Rubber heel salesman," Sandoval returned instinctively, preferring not to tell the truth.

"Tell me," the other whispered: "What are we actually supposed to do, if in fact the King … ?"

"Ssssh!" Sandoval hissed fiercely.

The winding stairway went on forever, leading them to higher and higher levels. Then an iron door swung open and they found themselves in a small room, barely able to contain their number.

Mawiras-Tendal disappeared through a tiny doorway. A second later he was back.

"Come this way."

They stepped into a much larger room, brightly lit. The Major assigned each man to his place. They were standing in a semicircle before a finely wrought door that opened outwards from the room they were in. As men do in moments of crisis, Sandoval found himself nervously eyeing every detail, no longer able to account for any of them rationally: the imposing marble fireplace, the ornate Renaissance table that bore nothing but a cage, and inside that cage a canary, the King's favourite …

Mawiras-Tendal opened the door, stood holding it wide, and announced in ringing tones:

"The Nameless Captain!"

In a silence haloed with mystery, a man entered the room. He might have been in uniform, but all that could be seen of it were the patent leather boots and high gold-braided collar: the rest could only be surmised under the large, white, theatrical cloak that covered it. His face was masked. For a few moments he looked at the conspirators in silence.

"I greet you, brave men," he said at last, in a quiet, almost ceremonial voice. "You have, every one of you, taken an oath of allegiance to me without knowing who I am. For that you have my special thanks. The time has now come for us to convert our ideas into reality. Within the hour the general uprising will have begun. We have worked on every smallest detail, and events will unfold precisely according to plan. Gentlemen, you are the ones who stormed the Royal Palace."

A frisson of delight ran down Sandoval's spine. They had indeed 'stormed' the royal palace, as people would later read. It was a shame, perhaps, that the 'storming' had proved so much less romantic than he had imagined. But he had learnt to live with the fact that life was never as colourful as his fantasies. Zizigan, from the look of him, was almost overcome by the fact that he too was one of the 'storming' party. The consciousness of it had so completely overwhelmed him that he turned pale and had to steady himself by grabbing the back of an armchair.

"The demonstrators will march past the palace," the Nameless Captain continued. "We cannot say precisely how the inmates will respond to this, or whether they will offer resistance. Your role will be to act as my bodyguard. Major Mawiras-Tendal will give the necessary orders."

Zizigan gave a deep sigh, and sank dizzily into the chair. The Nameless Captain stopped speaking and stared at him for a moment, then, as if suddenly remembering where he was, continued:

"Gentlemen, there is no cause for alarm. I can personally guarantee that not a hair of your heads will be harmed. This whole process is in fact nothing more than a formality."

Zizigan turned to the canary, with a bewildered expression on his face.

"Cheep cheep," he murmured, like a man on the point of death.

The Nameless Captain seemed about to burst out laughing behind his mask, and he quickly turned his face away towards Mawiras-Tendal. The Major remained deadly serious, his expression one of the refined disdain a gentleman officer might feel for the civilian volunteer.

"Now I must leave you to yourselves," the Nameless Captain concluded. "Be quiet, and patient, until it is your turn for action."

As he left, it suddenly struck Sandoval that the voice and enunciation were familiar. But no way could he recall where he had heard them before.

King Oliver made his way through to Princess Ortrud's apartment.

The princess had now resided in Lara for a week, but because of the general situation she had scarcely been out of the palace, and she was intensely bored. And yet she was very fond of Alturia and its people. Norlandians were invariably attracted to countries more colourful and exciting than their own, and those who had the means to do so were forever escaping abroad.

Since a child, she had always yearned for romantic Alturia, and now here she was, and they wouldn't allow her to go anywhere other than the palace park, where there were no fishermen in traditional costume to be seen, no picturesque cottages or folk dances—nothing of the wonderland she was so familiar with from her reading. She drew comfort from the fact that she was able to be with Oliver so often. She was sincerely and naively in love with him, as romantically as perhaps only a young princess can be.

Oliver found her in the company of Baron Birker, her country's ambassador. He kissed his fiancée's hand and greeted the visitor.

"How beautiful you are today, Oliver," she said, in a voice filled with emotion.

"And you too, Ortrud, you too," he replied absent-mindedly, and turned to the ambassador. "How are you, how are you, my dear Baron?"

"Your Highness, the people's behaviour is becoming more and more alarming. In the outlying suburb of Mahal, I hear it's come to violent clashes between the mob and some soldiers."

"Serves them right. Why do the military have to poke their noses into everything?" the King remarked apathetically.

"The university students placed a Boer's hat, in the national colours, on the head of General Mawiras-Tendal's statue, and unknown perpetrators poured tar over the image of General Larcas who put the revolution down. I'm afraid there could be further atrocities."

"I know all this, my dear Birker. The King's first duty is to watch over the happiness of his people. The inhabitants of my capital are indeed restless, but they tell me the excitement of the wedding will restore calm. But at all events I must advise you to go home immediately, and to lock yourself away in the ambassadorial residence. I'll make sure that my most loyal regiment, the Twelfth, is on guard at the palace tonight. So please, get back quickly: this is not the time for a gentle stroll."

There was no arguing with a royal command, even from so frivolous a king as Oliver VII. Birker took his leave and departed, seething with anger.

"Thank heavens you've sent that tedious man away," the Princess remarked. "I was already bored enough by your absence. It's horrible the way they keep me prisoner. At home I always had some source of amusement. I once had to inspect a hospital, and I was asked to open a flower show, and a sort of general assembly for a society for the protection of animals … "

"I'm bored too, Ortrud: let that thought comfort you. And I'm bored not only when I'm a prisoner in the palace, as now, but also when I open flower shows and animal protection meetings: in fact, even more so on those occasions."

"But why? I love to be out among people … "

45

"Me too. But not like that. Sitting on a platform, with a smiling face, full of envy for those seated below. I would love to be down there, Ortrud, right down there … among the people."

"But we could never do that. What would they say at Court?"

"Of course. So let's just leave it there. From tomorrow, everything will be different."

"Oliver, you're so impatient," the Princess remarked with a happy smile. "I too wish it was tomorrow, on my word of honour."

"From tomorrow, I shall be a different person."

"Me too."

"You too, very good. Why you?"

"But Oliver! Everyone says that marriage means a huge change in a woman's life … "

"Of course, of course. What can an unmarried girl know of life? And tell me, are you pleased by the idea of this great change?"

"At any rate, I'm very curious about it."

The King was lost in thought.

"Tell me, Ortrud," he began at last, "what would you say if we weren't married tomorrow? Would it grieve you very much?"

"If we weren't married?" she tinkled with laughter. "It's impossible."

"All the same … if something … intervened?"

"No. What could 'intervene'?"

"I've no idea. Some bolt from the blue … an earthquake."

"But Oliver … "

"Let's say, if the archbishop who was going to marry us dropped dead."

"We'd send for another."

"True, but as I say: just imagine that something … I don't know what … did intervene."

"I can't imagine."

"But Ortrud, that sort of thing has occurred before, in our history. Think what happened to Inax the First in 1160."

"What was that?"

"Inax was a really brave, seafaring king. He wanted to marry Borbála, the daughter of the King of Galazola. But just before the wedding—the day before—the ocean flooded, and a huge sea serpent leapt out of the waves and carried the girl off. Just imagine."

"And ate her?"

"It didn't eat her. It took her to an island and kept her prisoner there until they paid a ransom. But at the time there was a major financial crisis in Alturia, and it was many years before they could pay the full sum."

"But they were married after that, weren't they?"

"Not at all. The princess had lived with the serpent on the island for many years … and in the Alturian language the word for snake is masculine. So the princess lost her good name. They shut her away in a nunnery."

Ortrud was plunged deep in thought. The story weighed heavily on her simple soul.

"Perhaps none of it is true," she ventured at last.

"Perhaps. All the same, it's what every child in Alturia learns."

"That's not what I mean."

"What then?"

"Perhaps the princess didn't have a ... relationship ... with the serpent. And she never experienced the big change, the one that is so important in the life of a woman."

"To be sure," the King said gently. "And if something did happen at this moment—another sea serpent, for example, then you wouldn't experience that great change ... and I would never know just what a dear little woman you are." He heaved a deep sigh. "I would regret it for the rest of my life."

He stroked her head tenderly.

Ortrud gazed at him with eyes of love. The story of the sea serpent had thoroughly alarmed her. What would it mean if they really were forced to separate? Tears gathered in her eyes. Suddenly a great idea came to her.

"Tell me, Oliver, do we absolutely have to wait until tomorrow?"

"How do you mean?"

"Well ... I think ... the great change ... "

"What? You want to be my wife now?"

She nodded her head, shyly.

"In case the sea serpent ... "

"But my sweet ... I, er ... my *aide-de-camp* could be here at any moment. And you know what a stickler he is."

"So we must wait for tomorrow?" she began, deeply saddened. "Oliver, listen to me, let's not wait. Now, Oliver, now ... "

Oliver was profoundly troubled. Ortrud had urged him with such an adorable, naive charm, temptation stirred within him. Like other men, he wasn't used to saying no to a woman.

"But Ortrud, what are you thinking?" he stammered. "Such things aren't possible for a king and a princess. Of course, if I were only the president of a republic, and you were … I don't know … a shepherdess … "

"But my dear Oliver, it isn't only presidents and shepherdesses who … "

"Ortrud, just imagine, if the sea serpent carried me off and you were left here without a husband. We must be sensible."

"Yes, precisely, Oliver."

Agitated, the King moved quickly away to the window and stood staring out. Ortrud followed and snuggled up against him.

"Can't you see how much more interesting it would be today than tomorrow? We'd cheat the world. But how intriguing! I never realised how difficult it is to seduce a man. It's exactly the other way round in books. There it's the men who seduce the women."

The King felt wounded in his manly pride. To avoid having to answer, he drew the Princess to himself and began to kiss her. But all the time he kept a nervous eye on the clock over the fireplace.

At exactly nine a huge roar was heard down below. The King extracted himself from the embrace.

"Do you hear that?" he asked. "Do you hear it?"

"What?" the Princess replied, in a trance of love.

"They're here!"

"I can't hear anything. Who are here?"

The roar grew steadily louder.

"But can you hear it now?"

"Yes. Someone shouting."

"Someone, you call it? Shouting? Madness! Come here, look out of the window! It isn't 'someone', it's a mob, and they're not shouting, they're screaming. A whole sea of people."

"Holy God!"

"The entire population of my country is screaming outside the palace, and you say 'someone's shouting'. Don't be ridiculous!"

"Oliver … what do they want?"

"What do they want? How should I know? How would I know that, tell me?"

A mighty bellow made the glass in the windows tremble.

"Come away from the window, Ortrud! It's the revolution. The sea serpent!"

"Now you see, Oliver." the Princess said through her tears. "Why didn't you listen to me?"

When Pritanez reached the palace, after that memorable confrontation in the street, he darted into the porter's lodge, washed himself as well as his agitated state allowed, and dressed again as best he could, with the porter's help. The porter was a very large man, and his shirt and collar sat rather incongruously on the short, stout Pritanez.

"My, how you've changed, Your Excellency," the porter's wife solemnly remarked when she saw him.

But Pritanez was not at the moment concerned with the minutiae of personal elegance. He was looking for someone to whom he could pour out the bitterness of his feelings, and demand an inquiry. The first suitable person he came upon was Mawiras-Tendal.

"Major, Major … something unheard-of has happened to me."

"So I see," the Major replied, with a smile. "You had to leave the arms of your beloved so hastily that you put the husband's clothes on by mistake, or something like that … I'm sorry, but I can't help you."

"If you please! Do you think, with my social standing and figure, I make a habit of calling on mistresses? This is an entirely different matter. Major, I have been insulted. You must hold an inquiry, sir. It amounts to an insurrection!"

"What does?"

"Major," the minister choked, "they threw things at me."

"You don't say. This is serious."

"I think so too."

"I was referring to the state of your nerves. You must be very distressed."

"I certainly am!"

"Dreadful! To suffer a nervous breakdown in your hour of triumph! Because, you know, everything's perfectly quiet and orderly in town."

"If this is your order and your quiet … "

"You need a rest. Stay here until you can compose yourself. I'll catch up with you later."

"But Major! … "

The Major had already left the room, shut the door and locked him in. For some time he stared at the door in astonishment, then he began to yell and bang on it. But somehow no one seemed to be around in that part of the palace, and he yelled in vain.

Pritanez had not been the only one to take refuge in the palace from the menacing behaviour of the crowd. The Prime Minister and Minister of the Interior had done so too. From there they tried to make plans, and to contact the local authorities and the Chief of Police—but the telephone returned the engaged signal every time. They dispatched a messenger, who was immediately intercepted by soldiers of the Twelfth Regiment and detained in the building.

The government were sitting in the King's study, in a state of feverish anxiety and completely powerless. No one could say where the King was. Even the Major had disappeared. It was assumed that they had left the palace, taken refuge with the local authorities and were making arrangements there. But no one dared leave the building. From the windows they could see how the crowd outside had grown as night had fallen.

What was making them even more nervous was that, from somewhere inside the building, they could hear an indefinable sound—rattling, yelling, and then dying away—that gnawed away at their imagination: the sort of noise cattle make as they approach the abattoir.

"We should get to the bottom of this at least," the Prime Minister said. "Secretary of State Salvid, you must deal with it. Go and see who is doing all this shouting, and why."

"On my own?" the Secretary of State began, with horror in his voice.

He dared not go. Finally they all got up and set off towards the room where Pritanez was imprisoned.

By this stage Pritanez was quite beside himself.

"Major!" he was bawling, "Let me out. This is worse than being with a woman. I'm innocent. I'm innocent!"

The ministers looked at one another in amazement. Pritanez with a woman? Pritanez innocent? The man was clearly raving. Finally, with extreme caution, the Prime Minister unlocked the door, pulled at it, and immediately leapt to one side. The sudden opening had brought Pritanez tumbling out in a faint.

Four of them lifted him up and laid him down on a divan. They too were struck by the unusual size of the shirt and the collar that they unbuttoned at his neck. These totally incomprehensible details induced a sense of horror perhaps even greater than all the larger signs of a revolution at hand.

But their preoccupation with Pritanez was short-lived. He had barely begun to come to, when they heard the same roar from the square outside that King Oliver and Princess Ortrud heard from their apartments. Pritanez immediately fainted again.

"What was that?"

Everyone rushed to the window and gazed at the sea

53

of people outside the palace. The noise out there was growing steadily louder.

Just then the Secretary of State, who had been sent to look for the King, came back into the room.

"He's in Princess Ortrud's apartments. Come quickly."

They rushed out, abandoning the unconscious Finance Minister, and burst in on the couple in such great haste that all sense of etiquette was forgotten.

"Come away from the window, Your Highness!" the Prime Minister shouted from the far side of the room. "They can still see you!

Then the minister with responsibility for the press burst in:

"Your Highness: terrible news! They are demanding that you abdicate and hand over your ministers."

The ministers cried out in horror.

"Aha—duty is not a bed of roses," the King observed. "But what else can we do? I believe any resistance would be futile and dangerous. What can we possibly do against the raging tide of the people?"

"But all is not yet lost," the Prime Minister remarked. "The Palace Guard ... "

As if on cue, Count Wermold, the Colonel of the Guard, appeared.

"I am ashamed to have to tell you," he announced, "that the Twelfth Regiment, who were on duty, laid down their arms and went over to the insurgents as soon as the mob began to march."

"So there you are, then," said the King.

"But the house guards are still here," the Prime Minister

54

insisted. "They've got automatic weapons. They could machine gun the rebels from the palace windows."

"What are you thinking?" the King shouted furiously. "Shed the blood of innocent people? Who do you think I am, Philip II or the One-Eared?"

"With our life and our blood!" the Colonel proclaimed. "We'll form a ring around Your Highness and break out of the palace. Tomorrow morning I shall plan our campaign of resistance."

"My dear Count, a gentleman's first thought is not for himself but for defenceless women. The life of Princess Ortrud is by no means certain here. Your men must make that ring around her car and conduct her to the coast. There are Norlandian patrol ships at anchor off Bangar. You, Count, will answer with your life if a hair of the Princess' head is harmed. Take her to safety."

Numb with shock, the ministers understood that he was sending away his personal guard, their last line of defence. Ortrud looked at the King with tears in her eyes. She went up to him, and asked, in a low voice:

"Oliver, what will become of the two of us, you and me?"

"I did tell you, didn't I?" he whispered. "The sea serpent. These things happen every day."

"And now we shan't be married?"

"Well, you know, just now isn't really the time. We have to part now. Some other day."

Ortrud burst into tears.

"When shall I see you again?"

"Perhaps in the summer. Then, somehow … "

Looking straight ahead, and clearly troubled, he drew her aside.

"Believe me," he went on. "I shall always love you. Such things don't change. But now … now I have to find out what life is like, down there. Now go in good heart, Ortrud."

"God be with you, Oliver."

No sooner had she and the Colonel left the room than the Prime Minister dashed up to the King.

"Your Highness," he spluttered. "Don't give yourself up like this. It might still be possible to do something. Not just possible, but necessary. In the end, it's not just a question of Your Highness' skin but ours too."

"I'm sorry, gentlemen, but we must make every sacrifice. You did say that you would accept your share of the odium attached to what we did. Well, now you must make that good!"

Mawiras-Tendal entered.

"Your Highness," he announced. "The insurgents have occupied every place of strategic importance. I've just been informed that they have taken over the telephone exchange, the main post office and the railway station. Soldiers of the Twelfth Regiment have smashed the windows of the Norlandian Ambassador's residence. Baron Birker was hit on the nose by a stone. The question now is whether they'll take the Citadel."

At that moment the roaring, which so far had been heard at a distance, seemed to come from within, from the palace itself. The throng was much closer now, was inside, running from room to room. Everyone's face went pale, and their eyes instinctively looked around for somewhere to hide. They all knew, from their history books and from films, what it meant when the mob broke in to a royal palace.

"Stay where you are, all of you!" the King bellowed. "I'll shoot anyone who tries to run. Major, you go on ahead. I shall meet the representatives of the people."

Mawiras-Tendal left the room.

"And I must ask you gentlemen to do your best to put on a friendly face."

A minute later the Major returned with Delorme, Sandoval, Zizigan and the rest.

The revolutionaries lined up respectfully against a wall.

The King greeted them amiably and asked them to explain their demands.

Delorme stepped forward and began an eloquent, carefully prepared speech.

"We are well aware," he said, amongst other things, "that Your Highness was not to blame for signing this wretched document, but was led astray by your advisers, those wicked, incompetent ministers, whom the people will hold to account … "

Then he appealed to the King to prevent otherwise unavoidable bloodshed, and stand down in favour of his uncle, Duke Geront of Algarthe.

"Your Highness, don't give yourself up, and don't give us up," the Prime Minister shouted, then hid himself behind the Minister of the Interior.

"Dr Delorme," the King replied. "I am compelled to

57

yield to *force majeure*. You gentlemen must see that," he added, turning to the ministers. "I entrust the people to your care, Delorme. Take good care of them, with better fortune and, above all, with greater pleasure, than I did. I have just one wish: that you guarantee that my former ministers will not be punished for what they did. Appearances notwithstanding, they are human."

"Naturally we shall carry out Your Highness' wishes," Delorme said, most politely.

The ministers breathed a huge sigh of relief. Several of them went up to the conspirators to engage them in private conversation, assuring them that their own personal role had been a complete mistake: none of them had wanted to sign the treaty, only that wicked Pritanez. They all urged Delorme to exclude Pritanez from the amnesty granted at the King's request and to make an example of him.

"I've done what I had to do, gentlemen, and I must take my leave of you," the King said. "I should like to say 'till we meet again' but the expression is hardly appropriate for a monarch going into exile."

The Prime Minister came and stood before him. With great emotion, he ceremonially declared:

"Your Highness, at this momentous hour we ask for Heaven's blessing upon your journey, and promise that we shall always hold the memory of you in our hearts. You basically meant well, and to err is only human."

There was quiet applause.

"Thank you," said the King. "God be with you. Dr Delorme, proclaim my wishes to the people."

And he quickly left the room.

In that instant Sandoval realised why the voice of the Nameless Captain had sounded familiar. It was the voice of the King.

Sandoval's work was now very much in fashion. His sole exhibition was opened by Prime Minister Delorme himself, and all the leading lights of Alturian society queued up to commission their portraits. He was much sought-after, and profoundly bored. His lack of enthusiasm began to reveal itself in the pictures: faces whose pouting lips hung below their chins, eyes popping out of the heads, and heads that sat not on a neck but on an alarmingly elongated tongue. The extended tongue became a *leitmotif*. Houses, trees, mountains, all were painted with this elongated tongue, and above them a radiant sun or moon with its own tiny version of the same. Finding a way to incorporate the theme into seascapes proved more of a problem. The younger painters, under the spell of his glamour as a revolutionary, developed Tonguism into a full-blown school, though the thoughts of his bourgeois clientele whose portraits were done during this period turned increasingly to suicide.

Sandoval himself became more and more ill-humoured. Anyone who has breathed the heady air of conspiracy finds it hard to accommodate himself to the inconsequential skirmishings of the art world.

One day he returned as a guest to Algarthe. When the Duke became King Geront the First, he refused to leave his home. He would not be separated from his collections, and, because he feared they might be damaged in transit, he had been unwilling to move to the palace. That was now occupied by Princess Clodia and her personal court.

The Duke (now, more properly, the King) showed Sandoval his new acquisitions. He had been, Sandoval decided, a real gentleman, both moderate and discreet. He had not sent for the greatest treasures of the National Gallery: the Van Eyck still hung in its place. He had commandeered nothing excessive, just delicate little rarities, things that meant nothing to most people but were revered by the true collector. But he had changed very little. He took no more interest in politics than before, entrusting everything to the statesmanlike wisdom of his daughter.

He was now so far removed from events that there would have been no mention of Sandoval's last visit had he not chanced to meet Princess Clodia, who happened to be calling on her father at the time.

That she carried the burden of state on her shoulders, it was clear to see. By now Alturia's problems were not trivial. With the rejection of the Coltor Plan the public finances had sunk to the state of an intractable mess. At the Princess's wish Pritanez had been replaced by the chief accountant of a large bank who, a week later, committed suicide in a fit of book-keeping insanity. He was followed by a wine-merchant who fled the country without embezzling a single cent; then a business tycoon, who promptly arranged for his own denunciation, and a university professor, who simply disappeared, said to have

60

been lost in the labyrinth of the Exchequer and never seen again. After that no one had the courage to take on this ill-fated post, and Princess Clodia now handled the state finances herself, in ever-mounting despair.

But the moment she saw Sandoval her furrowed brow became smooth again.

"Sandoval," she cried. "Just the person I was looking for!"

Sandoval instantly assumed that she wanted to appoint him Minister of Finance, and protested in horror:

"Your Highness, I have embezzled every cent ever trusted to me. Don't put me in the way of temptation! There must be a few taller left in Alturia, though God knows where … "

"Now just listen, please! This is something else altogether. I want to send you abroad on an important and deadly secret mission. I can't use a detective. That would immediately give it an official character and there would be all sorts of complications. I need a private individual, and what's more, one who would easily understand the deranged mental state of the missing person in question—and find out where he is and what he is doing. In other words, I want to know the whereabouts and present doings of my daft cousin Oliver."

"King Oliver! But surely everyone knows that. First he was in Paris, then in London … "

"True, so far … "

"But then he joined an English expedition to Central Africa, hunting big game. He's been there ever since. We've heard nothing more, these past few weeks."

"Yes. That's what everybody thinks, and I have no objection to their thinking that. He slipped quietly out of the country, and when he returns no one will be the least bit interested in him. And it would be a very good thing if it were true. But I am quite convinced Oliver never went to Africa."

"Why do you think that, Your Highness?"

"First of all, because I know Oliver of old, and I know that all his life he has loathed hunting. In our childhood I was the one who climbed up trees after birds and used his pellet gun, while he cried over the poor little creatures I shot. Later on, when he was almost of an age when hunting was required of him by his rank, he always pretended to be sick when there was an official shoot. And when he took the throne he abolished hunting altogether. I really can't imagine why he would go after big game now … "

"This really is a surprise."

"On the other hand, he's so shifty and so unreliable—as his behaviour showed during the revolution—he's so devious that if he tells us he's gone on safari, and is giving interviews on the subject to the English press, then we can be pretty sure he's got something quite different in mind."

"Your Highness' supposition is strengthened by the fact that he seems to pop up in such widely different places. There are reports of him spending the summer in the Austrian Alps, and studying folk costume in Albania, and not long ago an American journalist spotted him in Kansas City, in his shirtsleeves: the King told him he was buying up petrol stations and living off the proceeds."

"Of course it's all fairy tales. I believed these reports myself, for a while, but since yesterday I've known for certain where he is. I had a letter from Countess Tzigalior. She says she's seen him in Venice. He was very much changed; he'd shaved off his moustache and side-whiskers, to look like an actor. Obviously, so that he wouldn't be recognised. But Countess Tzigalior knew him at once. And from all I know of my daft cousin Oliver, Venice is just the place where he'd feel at home."

"I can imagine that. A lot of people feel at home in Venice."

"Well, not me. The whole time I was there I felt as if I were walking around a sugary pink ice cream that was melting. Now, you're also the sort of man … so I think you would be just the person to track down his hiding place and discover where he's off to next. You see, I'm not entirely happy about him. Anyone capable of undermining and destroying his own claim to the throne can also be expected to try and get it back by some underhand and unpredictable means. We have to keep him under steady surveillance. He was just the same as a child. If you let him out of your sight for five minutes you prepared for every sort of catastrophe. You must travel to Venice without delay. Venice isn't as large as its reputation suggests. I think if you wander round for a few days with your eyes open, in the streets and on the Lido, you're bound to find him. Anyway, that's not my business. How you do it is up to you. All I'm interested in is that you give me a precise report on what he's up to, who he is in contact with and what his plans are for the foreseeable future. Are you willing to do this?"

Sandoval didn't have to think. Of course he was willing. He adored Venice, Alturia bored him, and right now this sort of irregular mission interested him much more than painting. Above all, he too was curious to know what the ex-King might be doing. Indeed, ever since that memorable evening when he realised that the King and the Nameless Captain of the conspirators were one and the same person, his imagination had steadily cast around for an explanation of the mystery. What could have brought the King to the point where—a thing without parallel even in Alturia's history—he could conspire against himself? Perhaps if he could find him in Venice, he would discover the key to the whole enigma.

"Talk the details over with my secretary, Baroness Fifaldo—including the financial details," the Princess added. "And don't say a word about this to anyone. Not even Delorme must know. Be as gentle as a lamb, and as wise as a serpent. This last point is the most important of all. And look to yourself, if you get involved with Oliver. Venice is not a nice place, whatever they say, and Oliver is bad company."

Two days later Sandoval arrived in Venice. It was now high summer, with few people—in fact only the natives—out on the streets in the heat of the day, the foreigners tending to stay out on the Lido, where he too took a hotel. If the King were in Venice, that was where he would be lodging, Sandoval reckoned—at the Excelsior. But after a single day on the watch he was quite sure Oliver was not a guest in that particular establishment.

Over the next few days he made no attempt to look for the King, so full was he of the joys of being once again in Venice. He wandered down the narrow little streets, beside the dark green lagoons, through the shady underpassages, making his way at last to the Grand Canal, where every one of the old mansions spoke in its own distinctive way to his painter's heart. He sought out the famous pictures in the Frari and the Accademia, travelled to Padua to pay a visit to Giotto, sat in the evening sipping iced coffee, and a little bored, listening to the music in St Mark's Square, met some old acquaintances on the Lido, bathed, and felt very much at home.

But then his conscience began to stir, and he tried to devise a system to achieve his aim. Princess Clodia had been perfectly right: Venice is tiny and sooner or later people must bump into one another. After all, where does one go there, if not to the Lido or St Mark's Square? Sandoval scoured these places systematically. He immersed himself in every square inch of the Lido, and stood staring with Argus eyes round the crowds of tourists in the little arcades around St Mark's Square where, by now, the whole of Europe was gathering. But there was no trace of the King.

After spending another week in fruitless staring he came to the decision that, if he had failed to find him in all that time, the King could not be in Venice. If he had indeed ever been there, he must certainly have moved on by now. He would have to extend his search to every city in Italy, which would be a great pleasure, if not exactly promising. All the same, he would have to try, and perhaps the Princess would approve.

He was sitting on the terrace of a little café opposite the statue of Goldoni, in a little square no bigger than a public dining room, writing to the Princess' secretary Baroness Fifalda to ask for funds and authorisation to set up a more protracted investigation. He was completely immersed in its composition, and caught totally by surprise when a heavy hand pressed down on his shoulder.

He looked up and was so astonished he leapt up involuntarily from his seat. Before him stood Major Mawiras-Tendal. And if the Major was here, could the King be far behind?

The Major had in fact followed the King into voluntary exile, making his way from Alturia independently. Oliver's firm wish had been to leave behind everything to do with his household and his entourage while on his travels. Only his *aide-de-camp* would be permitted to accompany him, and then not in an official capacity but as a friend and travelling companion.

The Major had changed a great deal since Sandoval had last seen him. He was, as always, a man of lofty, commanding presence, but once out of his soldier's uniform his military bearing came across as extremely odd. He had become a sort of concept. In his urge to conceal his officer qualities he had made himself altogether too summery, debonair, gypsy-like—and irresistibly comic. A royal tiger, domesticated to the level of a pussy cat.

"Sandoval, how splendid to see you here," he declared, having powerfully shaken his hand. "So, how are you, my dear chap, and what are you up to? Painting, painting?"

The chummy tone, Sandoval decided, though not the Major's usual style, must be an accessory to the costume. And his curiosity intensified by leaps and bounds. What had brought Mawiras-Tendal, nephew of the great revolutionary hero of Alturia, to put himself through such a transformation?

"I, er … you know … I'm here on holiday … " he replied. "I'm not painting at the moment, just having a look at the world. A man needs to, from time to time. But what about you, Major? Everyone 'knows' you're in Central Africa with His Highness."

"Sh … sh … " the Major responded, and looked round in alarm. "I … as for that … I'm actually here in Venice. Business, Sandoval. Business. You know, since I stopped being his *aide-de-camp*, I have business interests. But I'm delighted to see you here. Because, well, you'll see what a strange chance it is if I tell you that I've been running round all morning looking for a painter, drawn a blank everywhere, and now I bump into you. What luck!"

"A painter? You'll find plenty of those in Venice. The churches are crawling with them. Any hotel porter could bring you a dozen."

"Yes, I thought of that. But it matters what sort of painter."

"Ah, so you're looking for one with talent," said Sandoval, his face brightening.

"Well, er, not entirely. Rather, one who can be trusted."

67

"Trusted. From what point of view?"

"Someone who would be discreet; someone you could do business with."

"It seems, Major, you've forgotten, from the good old days in Lara, that I am very discreet, and someone you could deal with."

"Of course, of course, it's just that … actually, it's a question of your having to paint a Titian."

"A Titian? I don't follow. I do only Sandovals. You'll have to make do with that. Not a bad name, that."

"Look, what I'm saying … I know you painters some-times—as part of the training—you sometimes copy old masters."

"Yes, I did when I was younger. So, you need a picture copied?"

"No, anyone could do that. I wouldn't need you for that. What I'd like is for you to paint the sort of picture that someone who didn't know very much about art might think was a real Titian."

"Aha, now I get you. Hm … It could be done. You realise of course, the result wouldn't depend on me but on the competence of the person who views it. No real expert would be taken in. But then, who is an expert? What is the actual purpose of this picture?"

"You see, that's something I can't tell you, just at the moment. But does that matter, so far as the actual painting is concerned? Surely not. Look, this isn't a question of art; it a question of serious business. How much would you want for doing it?"

"For you, Major, five hundred lire."

"Good. I'll convey your offer to the appropriate quarters. And when could you start?"

"Tomorrow, I suppose. But my hotel room isn't really suitable for painting in."

"I'll give that some thought. So then, my dear Sandoval, give me your address. I'll call on you tomorrow morning and take you where you can create this masterpiece without anyone bothering you. I'm very glad I met you. Till we meet again."

The next day the Major did indeed appear.

"Good morning, Major," Sandoval greeted him.

Mawiras-Tendal became suddenly most serious.

"My dear Sandoval, this is where the discretion bit comes in. You must understand, and must never forget for a moment, that in Venice I am not a major. I live here completely incognito. None of the people I happen to meet in the course of the day's business has any idea who I am and what my role was in Alturia. They know me simply as Mr Meyer, and that I came here from Prussia, which accounts for my rather stiff, military bearing. Though, as you can see from the way I'm dressed, I do my best not to be too stiff and military. But it's not much use. You can't just wipe away all those years of service."

Having made his confession, the Major became visibly more relaxed, and less self-conscious than he had been the previous day.

"Allow me, my dear Sandoval," he went on, "to treat you as an old friend, as if you were still at home. Allow me to relax for a moment into my natural priggishness and stiffness. It would make the time I spend with you into a holiday. I need a break from time to time, or I could never cope with all this civilian ease and informality."

The Major moved with practised confidence through the tangled labyrinth of streets, while Sandoval quickly lost his bearings. Narrow little streets bent and twisted beside other narrow little streets, with the Grand Canal glinting every so often between the houses. They crossed over little white bridges, from one side of the street to the other and back, with the water swirling blackly in between, as if still heaving with the forgotten corpses of past ages. Sandoval had a notion that they might be winding their way through the district behind the Frari, but he could not have taken an oath on it.

The Major came to a stop before an immensely old house. In Venice every house is immensely old, as old as anyone can conjecture, in those long-forgotten centuries. But this house was not simply ancient, it was near-derelict. Sandoval was oppressed by the feeling that the inhabitants had not for many decades had the money to spend on a decent spring-cleaning.

"The Palazzo Pietrasanta," the Major announced. "Of course, it's as much the Palazzo Pietrasanta as I am Meyer."

But he left this cryptic remark unexplained. They went inside, passed through a courtyard, narrow but lined with columns, then up a once rather fine staircase to the second floor, where they came into a room that might, in Venice, have passed for well-lit, the windows not being directly overshadowed by any kind of building across the way.

"You can work here in peace," said the Major. "A colleague of mine will be here any moment now. He'll give you everything you need. And please, never forget what I said, about myself. And, you in fact … are no longer the famous painter you are in the real world. You're a penniless down-and-out acquaintance of mine, someone I picked up yesterday, and very glad to have a job. I'll explain all this later. Ah, here's Honoré."

A young man in black trousers and a knitted sweater had appeared, a cigarette dangling from his mouth and a knowing, cheerful, thoroughly untrustworthy look on his face. He spoke French, taking it for granted that every painter knew the language, a common assumption in those years before the war, when Paris dictated the tone. He addressed Sandoval as *tu*, in the popular Parisian manner.

"So here you are, me old dauber," he began, and held out his hand, smiling. Then he looked him closely up and down, frowned and turned to the Major. "What sort of toff have you brought here, old chum? Can he paint?"

"Of course. He's a very good painter. Had an exhibition in Munich. They bought three of his pictures, he tells me. What's so toffish about him? What do you mean by this … Sandoval, why are you all dressed up?"

"An inheritance," he replied bashfully. "I got two suits and a trunk."

"Ah, well … " said Honoré. "I'm sure Meyer has already

71

told you what this is about, though his explanations … The fact is, we need a Titian. It doesn't have to be as really swanky as if Titian had done it himself, but a good, solid piece of work, my lad. The boss knows a thing or two about pictures and he'll beat you over the head if you paint us a whole lot of trash. And don't put anything modern in it! None of this atmosphere, or contour, or vanishing point, or I dunno what! Well, you know more about that than I do. The sort of picture that a bloke, let's say some American guy, might think that one of the big dogs had painted in the old days."

"And are there any instructions about what I put in the picture?"

"Of course, I nearly forgot. A woman, holding a sort of dish. Because, you know, Titian has a famous picture of a woman with a bowl, er … a bowl of salad."

"Fruit salad," the Major added.

"That's it, old man. Everyone knows that picture. People think all he ever painted was women. You must know the one of the woman with the dish."

"Of course."

"So that's why it mustn't be the same. She must hold the dish on the other side."

"Fine. That's easily done. What about the dough?"

"Ja, good point. The boss says five hundred is a lot of money for a woman with a dish. Two hundred is more than enough."

"Two hundred?" yelled Sandoval, in a show of indignation. "What are you thinking? For a name like mine!"

"What name? Sandoval? Never heard of it. Anyway, this picture isn't one of yours. It's a Titian."

"But it's my work."

"Well, to show you what sort of people you're dealing with, you can have three hundred. Will that do?"

"It certainly won't. But I'm doing this for my good friend Meyer, and because I'm here on holiday and I've nothing else on at the moment. So, what's the advance?"

"My, you brought a real fussy one here, Meyer! I knew straight away you were too well dressed. My dear *maestro*, in our line of business there are no advances. We work in the tourist trade. We fleece foreigners who turn up in Venice. You mean to say that Meyer—such a fine, capable gent—hasn't told you why we need this picture?"

"No, not a word."

Honoré grew serious.

"I'm beginning to wonder about you, Meyer."

He drew the Major to one side and whispered a long rigmarole in his ear.

"Now, come, come," said the Major, with a loud laugh that strove for cheerful informality. "I'll put my hand in the fire for Sandoval. We can trust him absolutely. The only reason I didn't tell him is because I thought it better if you people did."

"You know what, the best thing would be if the boss saw him and talked to him direct. I can't take the responsibility, and nor can you. He'll be here any minute. Come on, Sandoval. And watch how you speak to him. The boss, you know, isn't just trash like you and me, or this Meyer. He's a genuine toff, a real gent. You have to call him Count. Count St Germain."

They found Count St Germain in one of the rooms on the first floor. He was sitting in a large armchair reading a newspaper. Seeing Sandoval, he rose and took a few steps forward, then halted ceremoniously and waited. He was a large-faced man, of powerful build running a little to fat, with clean-shaven, rather ugly, but wonderfully expressive features. He reminded Sandoval of a cardinal, a cardinal as represented on the stage of the Comédie Française. When he began to speak the impression grew steadily stronger: he spoke the pure, magniloquent French of the actors of that great theatre. From the very first moment Sandoval felt that he was in the presence of a distinguished person.

"This is the painter, Count," said Honoré. "Would you please have a word with him? The fact is, this Meyer hasn't told him what it's all about. It would be better if you could explain it yourself."

St Germain offered Sandoval a seat and the others withdrew. For some time he chatted politely about Venice, listening with interest to Sandoval's ideas about what mattered in art, and approached the real subject only gradually. He seemed to have been making up his own mind first, and speaking openly only when he had become persuaded of Sandoval's trustworthiness. Sandoval realised he had been weighed in the balance, and found insubstantial.

"My dear young friend," the Count observed, "you seem to be a remarkably sympathetic and straightforward sort of man. My unerring instinct tells me that we have nothing to fear from you and can admit you to our plans with confidence. We've just begun a major project whose fate will depend on certain crucial factors. We are in fact carrying out a patriotic duty. A patriotic duty to the home of every true art-lover, to Italy, or indeed, if you like, to old Europe itself."

Sandoval waited in suspense to see what might follow this splendid preamble.

"As a painter, you will surely be aware of the danger hanging over our ancient, our most venerable, part of the world. You must be aware of it, and you must also feel sincerely concerned about it.

"I refer to the threat from America. This threat is very direct—and I'm now thinking specifically about the way it affects us art-lovers personally. What I mean is, within a decade or two, the Americans, the *nouveaux-riches* of that brash new culture, will reach the point where they have amassed unimaginable sums of money, and with it they will want to lay their hands on timeless treasures of art. As you know, over the last couple of decades a new and in every way more dangerous type, the American art collector, has been popping up all over Europe. These people scour the most beautiful countries of our continent, and wherever they find old pictures for sale they pounce on them, snap them up and take them home on huge ships, to a country where they will decorate restaurants and other such vulgar establishments. Those pictures, in our opinion, are lost forever, as far as Europe is concerned. It isn't just one Guido Reni, Velázquez or

Murillo going astray. That wouldn't bother me at all. But what would be much more painful would be the great Italian and German primitives. And now they want to get their hands on the Holy of Holies, Titian. Fate has led one of these pirates to us, a certain Viking by the name of Eisenstein. He's made his fortune buying and selling shirt collars, or some such item of domestic utility, and now he's here in Venice, prowling around with the intention of grabbing a Titian. Now, our clear duty is to pluck Titian from the grubby claws of this American. In us he has met his match. The moment we realised that he was the sort of American who could never be talked out of wanting the great master—who would stop at nothing to achieve his vile purpose, but was prepared to rob and plunder to get it—we decided to mislead him in the interests of our sacred cause, as Dante did, when he threw sand down the throat of Cerberus: we dedicated ourselves to throwing a spurious Titian down the throat of this particular Cerberus to save the real thing from him. Do you take my meaning, young man?"

"Perfectly," Sandoval replied, with a smile.

"I knew you would. Now, I'm sorry I can't give you an advance for your part in the business. Just at the moment I don't have sufficient funds with me. The high calling in which I labour has made serious inroads on my fortune. You understand me of course, young man?"

"Perfectly," Sandoval answered, with a smile.

"I knew you would. And I can pay you only if our plans succeed, that is to say, if the American hands over the cash. But in that case I won't in the least grudge your two hundred lire, since you seem such a thoroughly sympathetic young man."

"Excuse me, it was three hundred lire!" Sandoval shouted furiously. He was now fully into his role.

"So, let's say three hundred, then. The reason I'm being so generous is that I want to keep you interested should any future projects arise. And, now that we have understood one another so splendidly, I must ask you to make a start on the work. I don't wish to press you, young man, but I'd be obliged if you could complete the masterpiece within three days."

Sandoval felt like a man into whose hand God had placed the trumpet of Joshua. He knew that by doing the picture he would sooner or later gain a full insight into the plans of the fugitive, self-banished king, which at present remained so totally obscure. He set about his task, and worked away diligently at his Titian masterpiece, without anything particularly memorable happening in the gloom of the bogus palazzo. He encountered no one but Honoré, and from him he learnt nothing of interest.

But as night fell on the evening of the second day, he packed up his things and, quite 'by chance', did not go back down the way he had come but got himself lost in the complicated layout of the house. He ended up in an unlit room, and was just about to open the door into the next when he heard the sound of conversation coming from it. The speakers' voices were very familiar. One he recognised as belonging to Mawiras-Tendal, and the other … the other speaker, beyond the shadow of a doubt, could only have been the ex-King.

Sandoval's heart was beating wildly. This was a chance he could not let slip. He instantly sank down into an armchair and closed his eyes. Anyone opening the door would think he had been sleeping there for some time. But the room was dark, and he reckoned he wouldn't be seen.

"I beg you, my dear Milán," the King was saying, "it really is about time you gave up this *aide-de-camp* manner. You've stopped calling me 'Your Royal Highness' half the time, thank God, but that's precisely why now, when you say 'old chap', it sounds as if you were piling every one of my titles back onto me. Don't forget, I am simple Oscar now."

"In that case, old man," the Major replied, audibly suffering, like a man forced to swallow some bitter mouthful, "permit me to voice a few concerns."

"Let's hear them," the King answered reluctantly. "All I ask is that you don't talk to me about the situation in Alturia. I've had it up to the neck. I don't dare to pick up a newspaper any more. These poor revolutionaries! That poor Delorme! But what can any of us do without money? It's terrible."

"That not what I want to talk about."

"All right, then. What?"

"I would like to draw your attention to the fact that Count Antas is on holiday here in Venice."

78

"Ah, the old idiot! Luckily he's no concern of ours any more."

"Not entirely. Tell me, er … old chap," he enunciated painfully, "what would happen if he, or anyone else, were to recognise you in your present—in our present—situation?"

"In the first place, they wouldn't recognise me, because I've cut off my moustache and side whiskers—they really made me stand out—and now I look like someone else; in fact, just like anyone else. And what, pray, is your objection to our present situation?"

"Well, you know … "

"I don't know! We're South American planters. Perhaps that's not a good enough occupation?"

"A good occupation? Thank you very much. It was a real idiot who gave Your High … you … that idea, my dear fellow. The moment we said we were planters people became suspicious. It's why St Germain's lot decided straight away that we were con-men."

"So then?"

"Well, so there was no point, if I might express myself freely, old fellow" (in his mind's eye Sandoval could see Mawiras-Tendal making a bow each time he mouthed 'old fellow') "in your making up that long story … "

"What 'long story'?"

"Well, how you diddled twenty-four locomotives out of that American railroad king."

"Look, my dear Milán, everyone shows off when he finally gets to meet the girl he's been skulking after for days. When I realised what line of trade Marcelle's lot

79

were in, I thought a story like that might be just the thing to help establish a good working relationship with them."

"I was just amazed that that old fox St Germain actually believed we were, er … in the same line of business."

"It's really strange; but you see, he did believe me. And that's the thing. For once in my crummy life something came off."

"But that's precisely why we shouldn't form that sort of casual connection with these people. I mean, the fact is, we have ended up as … members of a gang."

"And so? At least that way I'll really get to see life from below. That's what I've always wanted … and besides, I'll be able to be with Marcelle all the time."

"But I'm sorry, that situation has certain practical consequences, which do you no credit and could easily put you in danger. While I fully acknowledge Mlle Marcelle's feminine charms, and respect the intimate relationship between you two, I really can't approve, for example, of the fact that we have accepted money from St Germain. It's awkward, to put it mildly."

"You can rest assured that I'll give him all his money back, down to the last centesimo. But until then, we do have to take it, or Marcelle will become suspicious."

"We really must get away from Venice, before some really serious danger arises, some huge scandal that will hit the whole of Europe. Just think what would happen if word got out that the former monarch of Alturia had become a … con-man."

"Now please, Milán, you always look on the dark side

of things. You know perfectly well I have managed so far to steer clear of anything that might be called confidence trickery. But every woman calls for some small sacrifice."

For a while nothing more was said. Sandoval could hear the sound of footsteps. It seemed the King was striding up and down the room. Finally, he spoke again.

"No, my dear Milán, there's no question of my leaving, now that I'm at last beginning to enjoy myself. You won't understand this, because you were never a king. If I don't keep all that firmly behind me, I will never get to know life."

"Your Highness … I mean, my dear fellow … I can to some extent understand what you're saying, though for my own part I have never wanted to get to know 'life' better. I always had too much to do. What I don't understand is why you insist on this particular version of it. What makes you think that the Lido, and its idlers roasting themselves black in the sun, and this ancient Venice—something that escaped from a museum in an unguarded moment—and above all, this particular bunch of swindlers, are its true representatives?"

"Why? I've never given it thought, it all seems so natural to me. What would you consider real life, Milán?"

"Only something that would involve serious work. The military life, if that were at all possible. In your situation … our situation … I would propose serving in the Turkish army … where a chap can still find things to do."

"Perhaps. I think of life quite differently. Somehow I have always believed that the real test of life was uncertainty. Perhaps that is why I have always been so deeply drawn to

Venice. Here, the whole city is like a theatrical backdrop:
at times it even seems to wobble, and you never feel quite
sure that the whole thing won't have been whisked away
by the morning. Believe me, Milán, this is life. The life
of St Germain. This is real uncertainty, from one day to
the next. Maybe tomorrow we'll be rolling in money; and
maybe we won't have enough to eat. Without that level of
uncertainty … you might as well be a king. But that sort
of certainty I absolutely do not want. Holy God! To put
that appalling marshal's greatcoat on again! My worthy
cousin Clodia can rule in my place, to the very end."

Sandoval's instinct whispered to him that the dialogue
was coming to an end. Besides, he had learnt quite enough.
He got up and tiptoed out. But he wrote no report to
Princess Clodia about what he had heard, not that day
or the next. Some feeling, very hard to define, held him
back. Perhaps it was the solidarity of artistic minds.

Two days later the painting was ready. Sandoval made his
way down to the ground floor and there, in the great room
facing out onto the street, he found Mawiras-Tendal and
Honoré. He told them he had finished, and that it needed
only to dry.

"You don't say—finished already?" Honoré gloated.
"God knows what sort of rubbish you've painted."

"What do you expect, for what you've paid me so
far … "

"Ja, ja, just you be quiet. I'll go and call the old man."

Sandoval and the Major were left alone. The Major suddenly bent over to catch the painter's ear.

"St Germain is just now with a mutual acquaintance of ours, His Highness King Oliver VII … you met him one memorable evening in Lara. The King is living under the strictest incognito. Certain higher purposes have induced him to form a connection with St Germain, strange as that may sound. In the interest of those purposes—which I'm sorry I'm not in a position to disclose—it's very important that we don't give the secret away in front of St Germain, who has no idea of the King's true identity. I already know, from experience back home, that we can trust you absolutely. So, don't show you recognise him."

The next moment the King entered. St Germain greeted the painter affably and introduced him to the King, whom he referred to simply as Monsieur Oscar. He appeared not to consider him anyone special. The King seemed to know who Sandoval was and half-closed an eye, with ironic significance, in his direction. Then they all went up together to look at the painting.

St Germain immersed himself for some time in the contemplation of Sandoval's masterpiece, then he turned to the King:

"What do you say to that, my dear Oscar?"

The King tilted his head back and gazed thoughtfully at the picture, before murmuring:

"Hm. Yes."

"You see, what I really like about you," said the Count, "is the way you always express yourself so clearly and decisively, like a man used to giving orders."

Then he turned to the painter.

"My friend Oscar is a leading expert in the field of art. In his youth, if I am informed correctly, he was an errand boy in a large Parisian tailoring firm. He finds that the picture will do for our purposes. Of course it would be impossible to take him in—he saw immediately that it wasn't a real Titian: at best, the work of a pupil. But this Mr Eisenstein, the simple-minded Yankee we're dealing with, lacks the refinement to understand these things. My dear young friend, you may consider the picture as sold. Which, if I might set modesty aside, is no slight honour for you. If a St Germain buys a picture … What's more, if certain very short-term considerations didn't preclude, I'd pay you right now. However, I must ask you to be patient for a little while. You can be quite certain that your patience will be rewarded. Now, my friends, comes the conclusion of the business. Bring this shady American, this Mr Eisenstein, to me."

"Excuse me, Count," said Sandoval, "but the picture will need at least three days to dry."

"No need, my young friend. In the possession of my illustrious family is a unique process for treating paintings. It must be applied to the canvas while still wet: it will give it a patina several centuries old, and dry it at the same time."

Honoré and Oscar (as we must call our King, for the sake of brevity and a million other reasons) had over the past few days been progressively initiating Mr Eisenstein into the mystery of the painting. First, they revealed only that they had discovered some very interesting pictures in the palazzo of an impoverished old Marchese. Eisenstein showed an immediate interest, but was then told that the old man was very wary and would not allow foreigners into his home. For some time that seemed to be that. Then they brought news that they now suspected that one of the Marchese's pictures was a real Titian. Next they claimed that certain experts had studied it, and finally they showed him a certificate drawn up by an eminent authority. (That revealed just how far St Germain's contacts extended: in Italy anything was possible before the war.) Their handling of the situation made Eisenstein more and more excited, not least because not a word was mentioned of business. There was no talk of the picture being for sale; in fact, whenever he did show an interest of that sort they replied that they thought it unlikely that the old Marchese would allow it out of his collection. Then, very gradually, they consented to try and establish if the old chap would be willing to receive Eisenstein, so that he could at least view the masterpiece. The time finally agreed was that afternoon.

"My young friend," the Count said to Sandoval, "I should like it very much if you were to be present at today's memorable meeting. In your own interests, of course. Because when you next see me, as the proud but feeble-minded Italian grandee, it will be something rather special. And you can also help us sell the picture. You could chip in with the usual agreeably persuasive painterly art-historical mumbo jumbo. I like having people play the expert in all my ventures. It's so much more stylish."

Sandoval willingly agreed.

"All I would ask … " St Germain continued, " … is that, while in your role, you try to look like a reasonably elegant gentleman—shall we say, like an art dealer rather than a painter. The Eisensteins of this world don't think of painters as looking like you, and we have to use whatever means are suited to the taste and level of understanding of our clients. If you will allow me, I shall make you up accordingly."

When Sandoval returned to the palazzo that afternoon he was received by an elderly footman whom, after a moment's hesitation, he recognised as the Major.

"Sometimes a man has to do strange things in the name of duty," the Major said apologetically. "One day we'll explain the secret reasons to you, and we won't prove ungrateful for your loyalty. I shall now take you to meet the Marchese San Germano."

The Marchese was in the great room on the ground floor, sunk in the depths of a large armchair: an alarmingly ancient being in a grey, threadbare jacket, with huge spectacles, mouthing aloud the words in an old book, with the help of a magnifying glass.

"Who's that, Zacchinto?" he cried out as they entered. "You know perfectly well, my boy, we don't like our afternoon siesta disturbed!" This was uttered in a wavering senile bleat.

"The painter is here, *Eccellenza*," the footman announced timidly.

"Ah, the painter … ah ah ah … oooh oooh oooh … yes, the painter, now I remember," he bleated. Then, in

86

his normal tones: "Come in, young man!" And he leapt up nimbly and led Sandoval into another room, where he fitted him out in a scarlet waistcoat, bow tie, and a baroque wig of somewhat doubtful cleanliness.

"Now I look like a painter of the last century," Sandoval observed. "Isn't that anachronistic?"

"In these matters, it does no harm to go a little over the top," the Count insisted. "In our world it isn't enough simply to say you're a count. You have to wear a label on your neck and a nine-pointed crown with your title on it. It's not enough for someone just to say you're a king. You have to put a tin crown on your head. Our art is closely akin to the theatre."

"Mr Eisenstein has arrived," the elderly footman, alias Mawiras-Tendal, announced soon after.

Oscar and Honoré entered, elegantly attired, followed by a man and a woman. Sandoval studied both very thoroughly, particularly the woman.

She was the Mlle Marcelle of whose existence Sandoval had become aware when he eavesdropped on the conversation between the King and the Major.

"No arguing there," he said to himself. "His Highness has excellent taste."

Marcelle was a petite young woman, with a fine, piquant face and alluring figure, one of the type often called Parisian. Despite the fact that in Paris Sandoval had seen and known many women of this kind, Marcelle would still have exercised a special charm on him; but here, in this very different environment, she had a pleasantly refreshing effect, and he could imagine that she would be quite a new experience for the King, who, unlike himself, had not spent years in Paris. In her dress, and in the way she moved, there was something just a little coquettish.

"It seems St Germain was right," he said to himself. "In the world of the trickster you only believe it's a woman if her face is made up. Actually, if I had to choose between the two, I'd go for Princess Ortrud without a second thought. But then, I'm not a king."

Mr Eisenstein was just the sort of person you might imagine from his name: a stout, slovenly man with a large chin and nose, and a wide, sarcastic, self-satisfied grin, perhaps the permanent defence of a naive individual against the world.

"Marchese," Honoré began, in his rather weak Italian, "do pardon us for disturbing your rest."

"Not at all, my boy," St Germain bleated in reply. "Not at all. I'll carry on resting while you're here. It'll be just as if you weren't. I love young people. Youth … " he continued, with a dreamy, idiotic smile on his face. "Just come and go, make yourselves at home, just as you like."

"And permit me to introduce this gentleman from America, Mr Eisenstein, a great friend of Italy and of painting."

"Aw, yes," said Eisenstein.

"Interesting point, that," bleated the Marchese. "I've always thought so myself. Not that I do much thinking these days. Haven't for some time. Zacchinto, serve some refreshments. Make yourselves at home, everyone. Make yourselves at home."

"Our visitor is very interested in pictures," said Oscar.

"What's that?"

"Pictures, Marchese, paintings."

"Ah yes, paintings. Oooh, paintings! … " He rubbed his hands together. "Paintings. He should go to the Accademia. Some very fine pictures there. At least, there used to be. Perhaps they've all been taken away."

"The old boy's a bit obsessed," Honoré whispered.

"And maybe he's forgotten about the Titian. He's not all there."

But, very slowly, he managed to bring the Marchese round to the Titian. After a proper parade of reluctance he at last showed willingness to take them upstairs.

The picture was still in the room on the first floor where Sandoval had created it, hanging a little to one side, to signify how little the Marchese valued it.

"This is a very old picture," he pronounced without interest. "Lovely woman. Beautiful woman. That's why I keep it. Used to like those sort of women, once. Oooh, how I loved them. But I don't any more. Not any more."

Oscar and Honoré nudged Eisenstein in the ribs to indicate that this was the picture, and then gazed at it with expressions of ecstasy. Marcelle too did her best to assume the face of an art expert.

"Now that's nice," she remarked, turning to Oscar. "I'd be very happy to have one like that."

"And I'd happily buy it for you, my sweetest," Oscar replied. "But the Marchese won't part with it. I've already asked him."

"There's a painter standing right here," the Marchese noted, indicating Sandoval. "He likes it too."

Sandoval launched into his art-historical *spiel* on the subject of Titian's greatness. Everyone listened in devout silence.

Then there was a further silence, which Eisenstein finally broke with the long-awaited question:

"How much? *Quanto costa?*"

The Marchese made a gesture to indicate that he hadn't heard the question.

"Do make yourselves at home," he pronounced, without enthusiasm.

"You can't talk to the old man in that blunt way," Honoré whispered to Eisenstein. "I told you, he won't hear any talk of selling. You'll have to be content for now with the fact that you've seen it. We'll see to the rest, if it's at all possible."

"Aw, yes," said Eisenstein.

They took their leave shortly afterwards. St Germain, Mawiras-Tendal and Sandoval stayed behind, waiting on tenterhooks for what news the others might bring back.

"What's your impression?" the Count asked the painter.

"This American seems to be a real fool. I think everything depends on how far our friends can influence him. Particularly our most important friend. Even a blind man could see how much he fancied her."

"Of course," the Major agreed. "We got to know him through her, as her admirer. I'm quite confident about it. In my experience Americans trust women implicitly and do whatever they want."

"Do you think so, Mr Meyer?" St Germain asked, rather thoughtfully. "I'm not so sure. I'm afraid my instinct tells me something isn't quite right. There was something I didn't like about that shady Yank. But I really can't say what it is."

St Germain's instinct had been only too accurate in suggesting that something might be wrong. Oscar and Honoré soon returned, in a state of considerable tension. They had obviously had a disagreement on the way.

"So, what's up with our American friend?" the Count asked.

"Well, he likes the picture all right," Honoré began. "It hasn't occurred to him that it might be a fake. But he wants to talk the matter over with Marcelle. Tête-à-tête. So he's taken her out to dinner."

"So far so good!" said the Count. "Marcelle is a clever girl. She's brought off tougher deals than this before."

"Yes, it's just that this idiot," Honoré continued, pointing to Oscar, "I'm ashamed to say this in front of you, boss: this idiot is jealous!"

"My dear young friend," the Count returned. "I'm aware that you have this noble, chivalrous affection for Marcelle—you have never made a secret of it—and in other circumstances I might almost think of the two of you as being in the sort of situation I remember from my own youth … and I would not deprecate pure love, not even among our own little band. Plato himself observed that the army in which the warriors are bound by chains of love is invincible. But such feelings should never be allowed to get in the way of business. It's the basis of Kant's philosophy. I really don't understand you, young man. You're supposed to have been a long time in this game, and you certainly aren't the first admirer in her life. How could you permit yourself the luxury of feeling jealous? My dear friend"—flinging his arms wide and shouting—"my dear Oscar, I simply don't understand you!"

"I'm sorry, Count," Oscar replied. "but I can tell you most earnestly that as far as I'm concerned this game just isn't worth the candle, if Marcelle and this revolting slug, this Eisenstein … my God! … "

"It may not be worth it to you, but then I don't know what sort of financial background you have. My young friend, you must have been born a millionaire! We can't afford such eccentricity. We have to think of the group before everything else. And for present purposes, I am the group."

"But there's no point in talking about this," Honoré intervened. "Luckily Marcelle has a lot more sense than this idiot. She ignored the sulky look on Oscar's face and went off to dinner with the creep."

"Yes, I trust her judgement, and her very manly attitude," the Count agreed. "But I can't get rid of this feeling that something is wrong."

It was. The next day a sombre Marcelle arrived at the palazzo, where the whole company were waiting anxiously.

"The creep didn't mention the picture once in the whole evening. Whenever I brought it up, he immediately started talking about something else."

"So what did you talk about, the whole evening?" Oscar interjected, with fire in his eyes.

"What about? What do you think a man and a woman talk about?"

Oscar went white with anger.

"Look, Count, I think even you can see now that this whole business isn't worth it. I said from the start that the revolting creature wasn't interested in the Titian, he was only interested in Marcelle."

"Indeed he was," Marcelle said modestly.

"My dear Oscar," said the Count reflectively. "I very much fear you are right. I'm afraid nothing will come of all this. Or at the most, only for Marcelle. We can't interfere in any business she might arrange through her own efforts and enterprise. After all, we must all make concessions for the team."

"But my feeling," said Oscar (turning threateningly towards Marcelle) "is that—at least as far as I'm concerned—I do have a right of veto over her business … "

"My children," St Germain intervened, gently but very firmly. "You should never conduct your little love-games in public. It isn't the style. Look, I'm giving you ten lire. Take yourselves off to a coffee house and sort out your little quarrel, as young people must. I don't want to spoil the fun."

Oscar seized Marcelle's arm and dragged her off.

"Now that we grown-ups are alone," said St Germain, raising his hand, "let us spare a moment's thought for the young people now departed, and then bring this tediously drawn-out Eisenstein business to a conclusion. I think it would be best if Honoré and Sandoval called on him this evening and asked him directly if he has any intention of buying our wonderful Titian. I put my trust in your tact and discretion to get a decision out of him, one way or the other."

That evening Honoré and Sandoval met Eisenstein in St Mark's Square, where, like every other foreigner residing in the centre at the time, he sat over a black coffee listening to the music. He greeted them warmly, with a steady grin flickering around his lips, as if his habitual mockery had intensified a shade or two.

"It's just to hide his naivety," Sandoval reassured himself. But the bad feeling grew steadily worse.

After a brief conversation, Honoré boldly raised the subject. The Marchese San Germano was interested to know, he said, whether Eisenstein wanted to buy the painting, because someone from the Ministry of Culture had called on him on behalf of a famous foreign gallery who wanted to purchase it, and the Marchese, who came from a family of diplomats, was quite happy to let it go to the friendly foreign power concerned, only he felt he was now to some extent under an obligation to Mr Eisenstein and did not wish to part with it without asking him first.

Eisenstein's grin was even wider than before.

"I know what this is about, gentlemen, I get the whole picture, and I've been expecting the honour of your call. Of course the Marchese is under no obligation towards me whatever. He can send it to any friendly or hostile foreign power he likes: they must be queuing up for it. But please, don't get up so quickly; don't leave me so suddenly."

"Sir," said Sandoval, "your cool-bloodedness astonishes me beyond words. You're passing over the sort of chance that comes up once in a hundred years. Sir, a priceless Titian ... do you realise what that is? If the news of it got out, the world's top dealers would be marching in columns four men wide down the streets of Venice, sweeping all before them."

"And you can have all this for a trifling hundred and fifty thousand!" Honoré added. "Just think: the old fool hasn't yet realised what he's got there, and that's all he's asking. You could get ten times that for it, easily."

"But have I ever said I don't want to buy it?" Eisenstein returned. "Of course I haven't. I'll take it very gladly, and hang it up back home as a souvenir of Venice. There's just one condition. That Mlle Marcelle brings it in person to my lodging, at night. And of course not for a hundred and fifty thousand lire ... where did you gentlemen get that idea from? It's ridiculous! Let's say, a round thousand, and then I'm being very, very generous."

"But Mr Eisenstein!" Honoré snapped back. "You're mad! A genuine Titian! ... "

Eisenstein slapped Honoré's knee and grinned even more sarcastically than before.

"My dear sirs, I'm afraid you must have confused me with someone else. You seem to think, I don't know why, that I'm some *nouveau riche* gold miner or spice merchant who can't tell the difference between a Titian and a pile of crap. Allow me to present you with my card."

The card read:

*JAQUES EISENSTEIN*
*Proprietor*
*The Titian Gallery*
*New York*
*Fine art bought and sold*

The next day St Germain, elegant and refined as ever, was sitting in the foyer of the Hotel Excelsior on the Lido, and it was there that he heard Honoré and Sandoval's mournful tale. Oscar, Marcelle and the Major were also present. The bogus palazzo being now redundant, they had pitched camp on the Lido, hoping for something to turn up there. In those days everyone in Europe whose wealth had become a burden to them turned up sooner or later in the foyer of the Hotel Excelsior.

"So, let's bury this Eisenstein business as another great idea that turned out badly," the Count began dejectedly, but clearly intending to soothe. "We made an error, and to err is human. Let's say no more about it. The man isn't worth our thinking about. Do you know what this egregious Eisenstein's father was? A dredger man. The common or garden owner of a boat for digging up mud. A St Germain could never sink so low as to fleece the progeny of a dredger. My illustrious ancestor, the legendary eighteenth-century St Germain, swindled only royalty."

Marcelle listened with shining eyes, Honoré with mounting gloom.

"Ja, ja, Count, but what's our next move? They're going to kick us out of the hotel in a day or two."

"You are right, my dear chap. I've sunk pretty low, it cannot be denied." Then, in a suddenly changed, altogether unsoothing voice, he went on: "Nothing seems to work, my children. Nothing. It's the dead season. Business is slack all along the line. I don't know why we're wasting our time here on the Lido."

Oscar and the Major exchanged glances.

"Count," Oscar began. He was blushing with embarrassment. "Since I've played a part in the disaster … it would be extremely difficult for me to remain a burden to you, at a critical time like this."

"No more of that, my dear friend," St Germain interrupted, with world-weary *grandezza*. "My distinguished ancestor bequeathed me a miraculous instinct verging on the prophetic. When I first set eyes on you and Mr Meyer, some primitive impulse stirred inside me, as Socrates' daemon did in moments of crisis. No doubt my distinguished ancestor was speaking to me, whispering through the mists of time: 'Old man, I see something fantastic in these two fellows'."

Scarcely had St Germain uttered this remark than their fates underwent a truly decisive change.

A tall, bespectacled, clean-shaven man with a deeply lined face had appeared in the hotel entrance. The staff lounging in the foyer greeted him with the greatest deference. He went over to the reception desk and called out:

"If Paris wants to speak to me, I'm in the dining room."

"Of course, Mr Coltor," the maître d'hôtel replied, with a deep bow.

Hearing the name, Oscar shuddered and glanced helplessly at the Major and Sandoval. St Germain noticed, and was instantly all eyes and ears.

"Coltor?" he whispered to himself, entranced. "So that's the great Coltor!"

Coltor had intended to cross the room, but his glance fell on Oscar (or the King, as we should perhaps now call him), and he stopped, rooted to the spot.

"Why is he staring at you?" the Count whispered excitedly. "Perhaps you know each other?"

"Of course not. I've never seen him, and I've no idea who he is," Oscar protested in horror.

"Then why is he staring at you?"

"I don't know. He seems to think I'm the King of Italy," Oscar replied, with a forced laugh.

Coltor, believing that the laughter was aimed at him, smiled broadly and bowed in the direction of the King.

The King leapt up.

"Where are you going?" St Germain called out in dismay.

"It's nothing … just that … I have to make a phone call … " And he had already vanished.

But Coltor was even quicker. With a rapidity no one might have anticipated from so powerfully built a man, he overtook the fleeing King and declared:

"Your Highness, pardon me for troubling you, but

there used to be a most satisfactory business arrangement between us … "

The King's nervousness increased visibly. Taking refuge in his role as Oscar he rounded on Coltor in exasperation:

"I don't recall anything of the sort. You have mistaken me for someone else."

Coltor's normally impassive face turned to one of extreme agitation.

"But don't you know me, Your Highness? Even in this place I always wear the Grand Cross of the Order of St Florian you did me the honour to bestow on me, with your own hand." And he showed him the inside of his lapel.

"You are clearly under the impression … "

"That I am speaking to Oliver VII, the former King of Alturia. And I am all the more delighted by this chance meeting as for some weeks now I have been searching high and low for Your Highness—in Europe, America and even Africa. I have never given up hope that that we might still conclude the agreement that was so regrettably frustrated by the Alturian revolution."

"My dear sir," said the King, "I am very sorry, but you are the victim of a misunderstanding. I would be fascinated to learn just why you have confused me, a simple citizen, with the former ruler of Alturia, but at present I haven't a moment to spare. I am your humble servant, sir."

And off he dashed. Coltor stared after him, with a mixture of excitement and dismay, then shook his head and called out to the porter:

"I'm going up to my room. I shan't be dining. And no visitors."

And he staggered into the lift.

St Germain gazed round at his followers ecstatically, and in a low, deeply impressive voice, pronounced the following words:

"Ladies and gentlemen, that mysterious presentiment sent by my illustrious ancestor through the mists of time … well, it didn't deceive me. Like a saint plunging headlong from heaven in some old religious painting, it has come down to us, the thing we have waited for in vain for all these months—the great project. This could be the greatest deal of my entire life. I shall sell an entire country."

Mawiras-Tendal shifted restlessly in his seat.

"Don't say a word," St Germain commanded. "What, I wonder, can you possibly know, Mr Meyer, of the historical background to this scene just played out before our eyes? And have you any idea of what precisely happened in the Alturian revolution? I think not. I, however, am familiar with the whole subject. At the time I made a close study of an article about it in a Sunday newspaper supplement. But why am I telling you this? I shall now take immediate action. I shall go to Coltor and … but someone must come with me, that would make a better impression. Sandoval, you come along. Your hair is so dark you could be taken for an Alturian."

Mawiras-Tendal rose and drew himself up to his full height.

"Count … I must beg you … not to do anything, at least until you have spoken to Oscar … "

"Nonsense," he conveyed with a wave of the hand, and stepped into the lift, with Sandoval in tow.

Coltor could be approached only through a secretary who, even here on the Lido, worked feverishly day and night on his ever-changing itinerary. The invading force of St Germain and Sandoval was received with extreme consternation.

"Mr Coltor is not seeing anyone."

"We realise that. But we come in the name of Oliver VII, former King of Alturia."

The chief secretary looked at them as if they were mad.

"In the name of King Oliver VII? Oliver is in Africa. You … come back the day after tomorrow. I shall leave a note for Mr Coltor."

"Sir, at such moments in the history of the world every second's delay could be catastrophic," St Germain pronounced. With one stride he was at the far door and tugging it open. Sandoval was close behind him.

They dashed through two or three rooms, a posse of secretaries hard on their heels. In the fourth they found Coltor, pacing up and down in his nervous excitement.

"Mr Coltor," St Germain respectfully began, "you must tell your people not to be forever treading on my heels. Our business is with you and you alone."

"Who on earth are you?" demanded the astonished Coltor.

St Germain made a ceremonial bow.

"Oubalde Hippolyte Théramene, Count St Germain and Chief Steward to His Highness King Oliver VII

101

during his temporary sojourn abroad. And this gentleman is Baron Sandoval, His Highness' Groom."

"Out!" Coltor yelled at the secretaries. He had now recognised St Germain, remembering that he had been sitting with the King in the hotel lobby. "Take a seat, gentlemen. I am at your disposal. I trust you bring good news of His Highness."

Despondently, the secretaries withdrew.

"Permit me, sir, to assure you with absolute confidence that you did not make a mistake. You have a reputation across the whole of Europe for not making mistakes. And you were right again today. The gentleman you met in the foyer a few minutes ago was indeed none other than King Oliver VII."

"But of course it was."

"However, His Highness has maintained such a complete incognito here that even his closest followers still believe he is hunting big game in Africa. This self-concealment by His Highness has become, if I may use the term without disrespect, an *idée fixe*, and he refuses to give up his incognito at any price. If you wished to establish a connection with him, you chose the worst possible way when you approached him directly."

"Then what should I do?"

"At this moment, the position is that—setting modesty aside—the road to His Highness leads through myself alone." (Delivered with a deep bow, while remaining seated.) "Since leaving home, His Highness has lived only for the pleasures of literature and art and has eschewed everything of a political nature. Just between the two of us, the events of the revolution took a heavy toll of him. I open all his letters. It's quite probable that His Highness knows nothing of what is going on in the world. If perhaps Mr Coltor plans, or merely proposes, anything to do with him, I would ask that he refrain from approaching him directly. If he did, the response would only be negative."

"I understand, Count. I can well imagine it. But I must ask you to explain how it is that you and I never met in Alturia, or Norlandia, at the time."

"The explanation is very simple. I haven't been there for years. The connection between His Highness and my humble self is long-standing and dates from much further back. I was His Highness' travel guide and mentor when he visited the famous cities of Europe as a young man. I introduced him to the mysteries of life in Europe, if I might use such an expression," St Germain declared, with a wonderful smile. "Perhaps I can thank that for the honour he does me in regarding me as an old family friend. If he listens to anyone, it is to me."

"Forgive me, Count, if I, as a very simple man of business, change the subject rather abruptly. I am sure you must know as well as I do that Alturia has not been a happy place since the great change, and that all serious-minded people would wish to see Oliver VII back on the throne, and to conclude the treaty with Norlandia and myself."

"Yes, of course I know. As you can imagine, Mr Coltor, I have a hand in those matters too. Only today I had a detailed report from the *chargé d'affaires* there … "

"From Norlandia?" he asked, raising his head. "Perhaps Princess Ortrud is also here on the Lido, incognito?"

"Do you have the honour of knowing the Princess personally?" the Count asked cautiously.

"I have not had the privilege of being introduced to her. But I used to know her by sight, naturally."

"You are never wrong. The Princess is here."

Now Sandoval was becoming seriously worried. Where would the Count find a princess?

"My dear Count," Coltor continued. "We must keep in touch with one another. You say there is no chance of success if I try to engage His Highness in direct and immediate discussions … "

"None whatsoever. If you will allow me, I shall prepare the ground. When the moment is ripe I shall let you know, and the meeting you wish for will come about. Until then, all I would ask of you is that you do not reveal His Highness' jealously guarded incognito to anyone."

With that they took their leave, assuring each other of their immense mutual respect.

Sandoval was so astonished by the situation that, as they hurried back to the Count's lodgings, he could hardly speak.

"Wonderful, wonderful," the Count was muttering aloud. "I was right to listen to the voice of my distinguished ancestor when I first clapped eyes on this luckless Oscar. Now the royal game begins, Sandoval, the royal game. We're going to make a fool of the greatest swindler on the entire planet."

"And what will we get from this game, my dear Count?"

"My boy, at this moment I simply don't know. Believe me, we shall have all the time we need later on to think about these questions of material detail. Every second, hundreds upon hundreds of possibilities are flashing through my brain. We'll have to see which looks the most viable. But what matters is the beauty and excitement of the game, believe me, Sandoval."

They had arrived at the not very distinguished little hotel where St Germain was now lodging. Honoré was waiting for them.

"Well, Count. Anything to hope for?"

"I came, I saw, and I shall very quickly conquer. Bring everyone to me, my boy—that is to say, Oscar, Marcelle and Meyer."

The King entered the room, but not exactly in his Oscar frame of mind: he was irritable and bellicose. Mawiras-Tendal had already given him a clear account of what had happened.

"Count," he said, turning to St Germain. "Is it true that you spoke to Coltor?"

"It is. Today Fortune admitted me once again to her favours."

"And what was said, might I enquire?"

"You may not, my dear boy."

"My dear Count ... I have to say ... if you by any chance told Coltor that I am King Oliver VII, then everything is over between us. And I shan't be here."

St Germain stood up. His facial expression changed completely. At that moment he was a formidable figure.

"But what are you thinking? Do you think opportunities like this come twice in a lifetime? What sort of weak-mindedness, and folly, is this—that you don't wish to be a king?"

"That I cannot explain. It's a regrettable, but very old, I might say childhood, notion I have, that I don't want to be a king. Anything but that."

At that moment Marcelle ran in. She was clearly startled.

"What is it? What's happened?" she asked. "The police?"

"The police?" St Germain replied, with disdain. "Not an institution I am familiar with. Thanks to the inscrutable ways of Providence, my girl, our affairs have taken a decisive turn today. Consider this young man," he said, turning to the King. "You believe, my dear, that he is Oscar. But from now on he is no longer Oscar but King Oliver VII, the former ruler of Alturia. Whether you believe it or not."

Mawiras-Tendal leapt to his feet.

"My dear Mr Meyer," said St Germain. "I can see that you have already grasped our grandiose possibilities. From today, Oscar is the King and we are his Court. I am the Chief Steward, and Mr Meyer, who is so like a Prussian officer, will be his *aide-de-camp*. What was the name of that famous *aide-de-camp* of the Alturian King?"

"Mawiras-Tendal, if I remember correctly," said the Major.

"No, it wasn't that—but some such barbarous-sounding name. We shall complete our Royal Household with a few telegrams. Marcelle, my girl, you are Princess Ortrud, daughter of the Empress of Norlandia."

"Oh my God!" she gasped.

"Now, Oscar. Look at the way you're sitting there!" The Count rounded on the King, who had sunk deep into himself. "Is that how a king would sit?"

"No, sorry. It would be rather different. But, thank God, I'm not a king."

"Do shut up, Oscar!" shouted Marcelle. "If the Count says you're a king, then you are one, because he will certainly have his reasons why you should. If you say one more word, I'll slap your face."

Oscar fell into a troubled silence.

"That's the way to do it," said St Germain. "And to lend a show of plausibility to our roles, we'll have to lease the Palazzo Pietrasanta once again."

"But what with?" Marcelle asked. "We still owe part of the money from our last stay."

"What's this, my girl? I thought just a moment ago that you had complete trust in me, in my unfailing resource-fulness and hidden reserves of strength. Well, well: I must have been mistaken," he went on grimly.

"But I do trust you," she replied.

"And this is why. We'll pay for it by selling your diamond ring."

Marcelle clutched her left hand.

"Not that!"

St Germain turned to Sandoval with a sorrowful face.

"Groom," he began. "The history of the world fur-nishes us with many examples of enterprises of the most incalculable promise brought down by the small-mindedness, rapacity, short-sightedness and sheer stupidity of women. Now it seems we shall bleed to death, be utterly ruined and perish just a few steps short of our goal. I could say a lot more on the subject, but … "

Then, instantly changing his face and voice, he said, in the most natural manner conceivable:

"So let's have that ring, girl."

"Here you are," Marcelle replied, deeply moved, and drew it from her finger. "But I'd just like to know what sort of business this is."

"No flower will ever bloom for us in Alturia," Oscar muttered resignedly, his aggression having evaporated.

"Oscar, just you keep quiet!" Marcelle shouted. "What do you know about business?"

"As a reward for your readiness to sacrifice, my girl," said St Germain, "I shall enlighten you as to the nature of this project. It is not unknown in the newspaper-reading fraternity that Coltor has never given up his original plan. He still wants his Concern to get their hands on the entire wine and sardine production of Alturia. The plan failed to materialise at the time because of the revolution and the abdication of the feeble-minded king."

"He wasn't that weak-minded," Oscar muttered, clearly offended.

"But since then, the situation has changed," St Germain continued. "Under the new ruler, Alturia has proved unable to cope with its financial problems, and there are voices, steadily gaining in number, calling for the revival of the Coltor Plan. There is now a powerful Oliverist party, who want to restore the feeble-minded king to the throne. But the great obstacle in the way of all this to date is that the king has vanished without trace. Some people think he is dead, others that he has been seen in Budapest, with a feather-grass hat on his head, and others again claim to have spotted him in Kansas City, in his shirtsleeves. We now find ourselves in the happy position of having traced him and being able to put him in contact with Coltor; as a consequence of which, preliminary discussions can now be commenced in the usual way. That's what this business is about."

"I don't get it," said Marcelle. "Sooner or later it will become apparent that Oscar is a nobody, and we'll end up in trouble. Where's the profit in that?"

"Well said," Oscar chimed in.

"Marcelle, my girl," said the Count, after a short silence, "you are a fine, lovely woman, but, regrettably, you lack the spark of genius. You can't see into the future. You don't really think we'll wait around for all that to come out? Nothing of the sort. The whole game will last a couple of days. Just until Coltor presents a hundred thousand dollar cheque."

"But why would he do that?" Honoré asked.

"As an advance on the loan which will follow, to tide the King over his temporary financial difficulties. We cash the cheque, and instantly vanish from the city of lagoons. My friend Jacques Millevoi happens to be here with his boat at anchor ... I know a place in Mexico where they'll never find us. First you'll have to brush up your Spanish grammar. We'll need to stay there for some weeks."

"If I heard this from anyone else, I'd think it was a lot of … " Marcelle declared. "But as it's the Count … "

"Clever girl. I've done far more unlikely things than this before. The time old Rothschild actually believed the Pope had sent me for the two dogs, when my only form of identification was a panorama postcard of Ventimiglia … But now, my dears, we must part. St Germain needs his night of silence and solitude to work out the details of this wonderful plan. Come back early tomorrow morning, and everyone will receive his instructions. God be with you."

Our friends withdrew, Marcelle and Honoré fired with enthusiasm, the King and the Major deeply troubled, and Sandoval wickedly amused by the whole situation. Next, Honoré took his leave, and the others went out for some fresh air.

"Now listen, Marcelle," said the King, slowly stirring his cup of black coffee. "I have to tell you something really dreadful."

"My God! Are you ill?"

"Possibly. All I want to say to you is that I won't be playing the part of Oliver VII, ex-King of Alturia."

"What? And if I may be permitted to ask, why ever not?"

"Why not? How can I put it? … I do have my principles."

"Have you gone mad?"

"And then, I just don't feel I'm up to the part. Look, you said it yourself: as a child I never even had my own room, I've no manners, no style—you yourself told me no one would ever believe I was a marquis, so who the

110

devil would think I was a king? Especially Coltor, who has breakfast and dinner with kings every day."

"Wonderful! And why didn't you say this to St Germain?"

"I was going to, but then you shouted me down. I was afraid that if I even opened my mouth you'd make a scene in front of the old chap. And I didn't want that."

"Oh, I know how very refined you are. I always knew you lacked talent, that you're stupid, and you're a coward. You can think about that until tomorrow. Come to your senses by then, or you'll never see me again."

And with that she made her exit.

Only the Alturians remained on the scene.

"Gentlemen," the King began, "now that we're alone there is no longer any need to hide the fact that we have money. Waiter, bring us a bottle of good, strong, red Alturian wine, wherever you can get it. We must drink to the little scare we've just had." Then, as soon as the waiter had disappeared, he turned pensively to his compatriots.

"So what do we do now?"

"It's very simple," said the Major. "We're too late now for the night sailing. But we can be out of Italy on the first boat tomorrow morning. Your Highness has never seen Vienna. I strongly commend it to Your Highness' attention. Although, as it's summer, it might be better if we went up into the mountains … And Coltor could easily bump into you in Vienna. Perhaps Igls … But here, Your Highness' situation is one where only rapid flight will serve. It's like when you're dreaming. Sometimes the only way out is to wake up."

111

"Is waking up really the only way out?"

"At best, Your Highness might reveal your true identity to the group. But I cannot recommend doing that. Because if St Germain doesn't do it himself, then Honoré for one will try to capitalise on our little adventure. He'd sell the great news to the papers, and you'd be made a mockery to the world. Not to put too fine a point on it, Alturia would be a laughing stock throughout the world for years to come. No, Your Highness, there's nothing for it but for us to disappear."

"And Marcelle?"

"But Your Highness," he went on, with a hint of exasperation, "it's my turn to observe that, now we are alone, there is no need to hide the fact that we have money. At least, enough to take her with us, and to compensate her for any unfinished business she might have with St Germain."

"And do you think, my dear Milán, that she would come with us if she knew … if she knew that I am a king?"

"I know it for certain."

"It's not at all certain … And then again … My dear Milán, this is something your soldier's mind cannot grasp; she would be completely altered in her attitude towards me. Just imagine: she'd be respectful. She'd be afraid of me. And she would swindle me. She said herself that she diddled every one of her friends who had money. She considers it a moral obligation."

"She would never swindle Your Highness, because I'm here to look after you," the Major said, with a dangerous glint in his eye.

"But even if she didn't actually swindle me, her manner towards me would change completely. She would lose her waif-like charm. She would no longer talk to me as an equal. There'd be no more 'Oscar, what an idiot you are!' "

The King sank into himself, deep in thought. Then he went on:

"Gentlemen, I have decided. We're staying."

"But Your Highness … " the Major protested in despair.

"Not another word, my dear Milán. We're staying here. If there were any pomposity left in me I would say it was the royal wish. I came from Alturia to experience life from below. I can't run away now that it's begun to get really interesting, complicated and difficult. We must accept the strange situation we've got ourselves into. No great harm can come of it. So cheer up, Milán. Now the fun begins. From tomorrow I am no longer Oscar but the bogus Oliver VII, my own double. Who's ever done that before?"

When they arrived at St Germain's the next day they found the Count ten years younger. His great inspiration seemed to have filled him with strength. That morning he was on a level with the greatest of theatre directors.

He gave order after order. He sent telegrams flying round the world.

"This is to Baudrieu, in Paris—tremendous expert in legal jargon. This to Gervaisis, in Brussels—knows how to fall asleep during conversation in the grand aristocratic

113

manner. And this to Valmier, the perfect flunkey. We must bring them all together, the very best in their professions: at this stage we really can't consider expense or effort. Which reminds me. Honoré, nip round to Mr Beetz in the hotel next door and sell him Marcelle's ring. We need some petty cash."

Marcelle heaved a painful sigh.

"Then carry straight on and hire the Palazzo Pietrasanta—the royal residence. Sandoval, you go and get an Alturian flag. Two gold sardines on a field of silver. If you can't buy one, have one made. Meyer, on you falls the important duty of intellectual preparation. We need all the information we can get about Alturia and its half-witted king. In particular, we must dig up illustrated news sheets from the time of the revolution. We absolutely must locate a portrait of Princess Ortrud. Marcelle, take yourself off to one of the larger jewellers in the Merceria. Ask him to bring his collection to the Pietrasanta. We shall want something nice and showy … perhaps a pendant … yes, that'll be best … which King Oliver is to present as a token of his love to Princess Ortrud. Then, my girl, you must find us one of those toothpaste advertisements with the king brushing his teeth."

"What's that for?" she asked in stupefaction.

"No questions, my girl. Just be on your way, and good luck to you."

The team raced off for the next boat to town, to carry out his commissions.

"And me?" said Oscar, now finding himself alone with St Germain.

"You stay here. Now we get to the difficult bit. Come, my young friend, we'll take a little walk on the seafront. This is the place where Goethe so memorably heard the fishermen singing to one another across the water, answering one another with alternate lines from *Jerusalem Delivered*. I feel like singing myself. Perhaps the setting will inspire us both."

When they reached the Lungomare—the seafront promenade—St Germain began his little speech:

"Now listen carefully, my young friend. I've something serious to say to you. You are not yet ready for your role."

"I've already told you," Oscar replied glumly. "I'm resigned to the inevitable."

"I'm not talking about that. I've never doubted for a moment that you would do it. You must have at least that much common sense. The only question now is, can you actually play the part? Do you know how to live, what to do, to be a king?"

"Well, I haven't thought much about it."

"I knew it. That's the trouble. A good actor must have an intimate knowledge of the person he has chosen to present. And he must fully understand the greatness inherent in the role. You must rouse some enthusiasm in yourself. It's the only way we'll get anywhere near our still very distant goal. That's what I want to talk to you about, my young friend."

"Now look, Count … "

"Yes, yes, yes. Don't say a word, just listen. You have a very good-hearted, direct manner, and in general that's an admirable quality. You know how to make yourself popular with everyone you meet. I'm rather fond of you myself. But it's not what we need now. A king isn't required to be a human being, like everyone else. He must be the sort of human being who can inspire his contemporaries with awe and wonder. You see, in the long, hard year that is the life of the ordinary man, the king is a red-letter day. A holiday. A lifting up of eyes in adoration to the sky. There have been great kings who achieved fame by destroying enemies abroad, and great kings who cared about the sort of chickens the peasantry cooked in their saucepans. But none of that matters; it's not the point. Deeds and good intentions don't confer royalty. The king fulfils his duty as a great man simply by being. Anyone can win praise for his acts and achievements: the sole duty of a king is to exist in the world. Like a mountain. My young friend, plains can be cultivated, ships can be carried on the backs of rivers, but mountains are the only things that rise, tall and silent, above the plains, rivers and nations of the world. They simply stand there, and their existence directs man's attention to his eternal values. If there were no mountains, and no kings, my young friend, people would think that everything in the world was flat, something merely to be exploited. A king exists to draw his people's attention to the pure air of the peaks and the heights of destiny. He is a legend incarnate, the one great comfort and reassurance. That alone does more good for the country than fifty military barracks. It is a greater source of strength than fifty battleships. And for him to raise a nation to the heights of destiny he needs do nothing more than to emanate that strange, merciful gift we call royalty. There was a medieval Hungarian king who went into the enemy camp with a stick in his hand and led his rebellious brother out of it into captivity, solely by exercising his royalty … So look to yourself, young man! Are you standing here, like a cloud-capped mountain peak, like a king? Think about it. God be with you."

For some time the King remained alone, pacing up and down the promenade, deep in thought. Here Goethe had once stood listening to the fishermen's song; now visitors in beachwear raced across the sand down to the sea. But lost in his inner musings he failed to notice them. He pondered, and felt ashamed. St Germain had been the first person ever to explain to him what it meant to be king.

Sandoval 'enjoyed' a daily post-prandial siesta in the ghastly little hotel room, whose window had been some-how designed to have no actual view.

"My God, the things I do for Alturia!" he mused. "Here I am, in this smelly, airless hole, where I wake every single morning swollen to twice my normal size, thanks to the attentions of my friends the mosquitoes, and go down to the street like a pauper, or someone covered in ringworm, or tattoos … And then, the money I had from Princess Clodia, and I haven't written her a single word … to think I could be staying in some grand hotel enjoying the choicest fish and *frutti di mare* instead of badly prepared *pasta asciutta* … "

There was a knock at the door. Mawiras-Tendal came in.

"Forgive me for troubling you," he began anxiously. "I need to speak with you urgently."

"At your service, Major."

"Sandoval, it must be as obvious to you as it is to me, that we have to do something. We can't allow this business to carry on. His Highness' unfortunate compliance is going to make him a permanent laughing stock in the eyes of the world. The ex-king consorting with swindlers. It's dreadful to think what the papers will make of it! We must do something urgently."

"You are right, Major. But what?"

"Look, Sandoval, we both come from old conspiratorial families. We must be able to find a neat solution. Now, I've got an idea. You should know that Count Antas, the former royal chief steward, is here in Venice."

"Antas, that old buffoon? The one I spirited away just before the revolution?"

"The same. We must use him as our instrument."

"Why him?"

"Because I can't do anything myself. The King must never know of my part in this business. Antas will have to be persuaded that someone here in Venice is playing confidence tricks in His Highness' name, and that he has a duty to put a stop to it by alerting Coltor and putting him on his guard. What makes it all the better is that Coltor knows Antas and will believe him. What do you think of the idea?"

"Hm."

"Well, I think it's the best solution. I'll write to him straight away. Do you have any suitable paper? Thanks. First we'll compose the letter, then I'll take it and type it up in the hotel writing room. Should I write anonymously? No, it'll be better if I forge the signature of some well-known Alturian. That'll be more convincing. So, let's see now … "

And he composed the following letter:

*Most respected Count,*

*I appreciate that you are in Venice* procul negotiis, *hoping to enjoy a little freedom from worry after these last very difficult months, and I hesitate to trouble you with questions of state and politics. But this is a matter calculated to stir up the blood of every true Alturian, one that is impossible for us to look upon and still stand idly by. It is above all your professional duty to put a stop to these corrupt and wicked practices. I respectfully bring to your attention the following lines, in which I briefly describe certain outrageous events taking place here in Venice.*

*You should know, Your Excellency, that Coltor has been residing on the Lido for the past few days. He has never given up the hope—as I believe you never have—that Oliver VII should one day return to his ancestral throne and bring salvation to his country by signing the proposed treaty.*

*Coltor's hopes have somehow come to the knowledge of an international adventurer calling himself Count St Germain. This fraudster has conceived the notion of hiring someone with a highly deceptive resemblance to King Oliver, differing from him only in the lack of moustache and sideburns—which this St Germain explains as having been shaved off by the King to preserve his incognito. The villain has also presumed to put up other suitably plausible members of the Royal Household, a bogus Major Mawiras-Tendal among them, and who knows when an equivalent Count Antas might appear?*

*Coltor, at least from appearances so far, has gone along with all this. The royal impersonation is so perfect that it has already imposed on this highly intelligent Norlandian. St Germain is now about to take his next major step and bring Coltor and the 'king' together, in the hope of making a great deal of money out of the deluded entrepreneur.*

*Count, this is not something from which you can stand aside. You cannot, because the resulting scandal will cause endless difficulty for His Highness personally and for the whole of Alturia. You cannot stand aside, because Coltor is our true friend, and will certainly prove grateful to the man who rescues him from the claws of swindlers by exposing them.*

*While it would give me the greatest pleasure to leap into action myself, I am not someone Coltor knows and he might well decline to believe me. It would have much greater force if you, who are so very well known and respected by the man, were personally to remove the scales from his eyes.*

*The situation, dear Count, calls for instant action. St Germain intends to set up this meeting in the very near future. We must not fail to act. I would like to suggest that you write Coltor a preliminary letter and call on him immediately afterwards, at the Hotel Excelsior, for further discussion.*

*I beg you again, in the name of Alturia and in your own interests, to step onto the field of battle without delay.*

*Your respectful adherent*

*Dr Palawer (former State Secretary for Transport)*

"There we are," said the Major. "If you'd just let me have that sheet of paper, I'll type it up and take it to the Hotel Bonvecchiati myself. It was quite by chance that I discovered he was staying there. Sandoval, this is the very first time I ever have been disloyal to His Highness, but there are times when betrayal is the truest mark of loyalty."

Left to himself, Sandoval got up, put on his coat and went down to the seafront to think. The Major's course of action did not please him in the slightest. He was in Venice as the trusted emissary of Princess Clodia, of Delorme and, more generally, of the victorious revolution. As recently as yesterday it had been clear to him that he could only serve their cause by joining in the King's little game. If they could entrap Coltor, the whole affair would then come to light in all its ridiculousness. That could only be of advantage, in one of two ways. On the one hand, it might compromise Coltor and the whole treaty and thus prevent the latter ever becoming reality, perhaps at the same time destroying any desire on Coltor's part to attempt similar experiments. On the other, now that he had got to know Oliver and to understand the motives behind his actions, Sandoval felt that he might still make use of the situation to the King's advantage. True, if it came to light that Oliver had personally taken part in such an inappropriate and foolish game, it would make a return to his ancestral throne much more difficult, perhaps impossible—but then the King feared nothing so much as going back. Perhaps it really wouldn't bother him at all if these events made him seem an even more bohemian type, and even more of an enigma, in the public eye—in fact, the role he had chosen to play was probably quite close to his heart.

But then, Mawiras-Tendal's intervention might not only put an end to St Germain's plans but also to his own expectations. But how could he stop it? It seemed impossible. By now the letter would undoubtedly have been written and delivered. All he could hope for would be to take some sort of step to mitigate its effect. It was lucky the Major had not been able to keep his thoughts to himself but had shared them with him. But what could he do? Either stop Antas going to Coltor, or prevent Coltor giving credence to Antas' words. But how?

Sandoval was not a man to spend much time in contemplation. He was one of those people who always act on the immediate impulse, and then have no idea what they are doing. He had one positive fact to go on: that Antas was here in the city, in the Hotel Bonvecchiati. Minutes later, he was sitting in a boat and drawing alongside the Riva dei Schiavoni.

He made his way through St Mark's Square, passed under the arch of the Oratorio, through the Merceria and into the Calle dei Fabri, where all the little jewellers were. Here he bumped into Marcelle. For the first time he noticed what a very attractive girl she was. "Not the sort of beauty you'd notice indoors," he thought, "but one of those girls who really stand out in a street … "

Marcelle explained what had passed at the jeweller's, and the other errands she had been running for St Germain. Together they made their way back to St Mark's.

"Tell me, Sandoval," she asked. "What do you think of all this?"

"Pure genius," he replied. "A plan like that occurs to the human brain once in a hundred years."

"Do you think so? To me it all seems too perfect. To be perfectly frank, these big projects leave me cold. I'd much prefer some ... some decent, responsible old guy in whose company I could relax. You don't happen to know of anyone?"

"I'll think about it. And what about Oscar? Oscar is horribly jealous."

"True. But isn't it wonderful? For a man, in this day and age, to be jealous of a woman ... perhaps that's why I'm so fond of him, and why I forgive him his stupidity and dullness ... I've seldom met such a cack-handed bloke in my life."

They were now standing on the embankment opposite the tall, slender tower of San Giorgio Maggiore, looking out at the marine panorama that, before the war, every human being worth the name gazed on once in his lifetime, like a Muslim on pilgrimage to Mecca. Though he had seen it a hundred times, Sandoval now gave himself up fully to the roseate loveliness of the Venetian scene. Just then a large, white-painted boat glided slowly by on the golden water of twilight, on its way to anchor somewhere beside the church of Santa Maria della Salute. And that boat, on its mysterious journey, gave Sandoval the great idea that he had been searching for the whole afternoon.

"Marcelle," he shouted, "I have it. I've found someone for you!"

"Who's that?"

"A wonderful old pasha, the greatest buffoon on the entire planet! He's simply made for you. He's here in Venice. You must get onto him straight away. I have his address."

"Now look here, chum. You're not going to drag me down that road!" she protested, bristling with moral indignation. "You must learn to give people their due. Do you think I'm some sort of tart? That I want that sort of relationship? Certainly not. Listen, boy, my relationships last at least a fortnight. Some have been a lot longer."

"God help me, my precious, but I had no such thought," he replied by way of apology. "I know very well who I'm talking to. Listen, I'm a portrait painter, I can tell the difference between one woman and another. We'll just be putting on a little show. Now, let's first go and have dinner."

They wined and dined very pleasantly in a little restaurant just off St Mark's. When they had finished they returned to the Square.

St Mark's Square is the centre of the world. Before the war broke out, the world was much smaller than it is now, and there were far fewer people; that is to say, fewer people who counted as such. There were just one or two locations that could claim to be such centres, on the grounds that at some time or other 'everyone' ended up strolling around them. St Mark's was certainly one of these.

Sandoval had calculated correctly. They did indeed meet Antas, and in the most fortunate of circumstances. The Count was alone, ambling around the piazza in a pair of black-and-white chequered trousers and white linen jacket, with an imposing carnation in his buttonhole, and eyeing the ladies through his monocle with a degree of interest that belied his age. Sandoval made sure they approached along his line of vision. As they drew closer, Antas became so overwhelmed by admiration for Marcelle that he failed to notice the painter, until his loud and enthusiastic greeting:

"Good evening, Count."

Antas was horribly startled, but, recognising Sandoval, his astonished face was transformed into a happy smile and he advanced towards the two of them.

"Oh, Sandoval! Forgive me for troubling you, but I really can't pass over the opportunity of having a couple of words with you … here in St Mark's Square … " (bowing furiously all the while in Marcelle's direction, and leaving no doubt why he was so very delighted to meet him).

"*Chère* Marcelle," said Sandoval, "allow me to introduce my most distinguished patron Count Antas, former Royal Chief Steward to King Oliver VII."

Marcelle smiled a very friendly smile, and a lively conversation started between the two. At Antas' suggestion, they took a seat in one of the cafés. Sandoval listened with half an ear to the Count's naive bragging while he considered what to do. He gathered from what was being said that the Count had left his hotel soon after lunch and had not been back since. Perhaps he hadn't yet had the Major's letter. By the next morning, when he did get it, he would be on the very best of terms with Marcelle.

Suddenly he could refrain no longer from asking him:

"Count, forgive me if I presume on our old intimacy to

125

ask: what did Her Ladyship say when you returned home after our last little outing?"

"Ah, my boy, I had a stroke of luck. Enormous luck. By the time I got home the revolution had broken out and I was relieved of my duties. And then it really played havoc with her nerves. She forgot about everything else. The poor thing has never recovered from the disaster. That's why I came to Venice for a break."

Marcelle explained that she too was a painter, though not one who needed to work. She was in Venice on a study trip. And she adored seafood. She spoke in a refined, distinguished way, to Sandoval's delight. They took their leave of Antas towards midnight, having planned a trip for the following day to the little fishing village on Burano, whose colourful boats and lively water-life Marcelle would be sure to find interesting.

In the boat going back she said: "Tell me, is he a real count?"

"Absolutely the real thing. And his grandfather before him."

"Yes, it showed. Such a fine gentleman. Not like that poor Oscar. But that's why I love Oscar all the more. Now why would that be?"

"Like attracts like."

"Quite probably."

St Germain was still up when they called round to tell him what had been happening. Naturally they said no more than what was necessary, and did not implicate Mawiras-Tendal. Sandoval said that he just happened to know this Palawer person who had written the letter: he had been in his company on several occasions in France and they had now met again in Venice.

"Chance events are always interesting," was St Germain's response. "What we need to establish now is how this Palawer knew about our plans. Do you have any suggestions?"

Sandoval had the feeling he was being cross-examined. But he had come prepared for the question.

"All I can think is someone in Coltor's entourage has been blabbing about what an amazing deal his boss is working on. And of course Palawer, as an Alturian, would have known that the King isn't in Venice, so Coltor could only be dealing with an impostor."

"Hm. Are you so sure the King isn't in Venice?"

Sandoval began to feel rather uncomfortable. Did this man actually suspect something? Was his illustrious ancestor whispering something to him through the mists of ages?

"Of course I'm sure," he replied. "The King is hunting big game in Central Africa."

"So they say," said St Germain, thoughtfully. "Oh well, no matter. Perhaps tomorrow … "

And he reworked the details of the rest of the plan, taking Antas into account.

Early next morning they set off for Burano.

Sandoval had arranged a particularly early rendezvous so that Antas would not have time to call on Coltor beforehand. When they met, the Count appeared rather agitated, as if something were weighing heavily on his mind. Obviously Mawiras-Tendal's letter, which he must have now read.

Once they were sitting in the boat and heading out over the unruffled water towards the ring of tiny islands that encircle the city, Antas could restrain himself no longer and poured out his troubles.

"I had a letter this morning, from a certain Dr Palawer, a former Secretary of State in my homeland, Alturia," he began. "He tells me there are swindlers on the prowl, here in Venice, passing themselves off as King Oliver VII and his royal household. They hope to take in the great financier Coltor. The whole story is so improbable that I would never have believed it if anyone other than Palawer had told me. And the most outrageous thing of all, he says, is that one of the gang is preparing to impersonate me. Calling himself Count Antas … it's monstrous! Just imagine, Sandoval, if my wife heard that I was consorting with swindlers! I'd never be able to set foot in Alturia again."

"And what do you intend doing about it, Count?"

"I'll go to Coltor later today, show him the letter, and expose the whole ungodly business."

"Today? I thought we might have the whole day together," whimpered Marcelle. "I thought we were going out to Burano."

"Oh, how wonderful you are," Antas enthused. "How happy I would be, my God, how happy I would be, if we could stay there … "

He wavered for a moment, then heaved a profound sigh.

"Duty is not a bed of roses, as our national poet tells us. I really must speak with Coltor today. Who knows, tomorrow may be too late. Sometimes you can be taken in so quickly you hardly even notice."

"Then at least let me go with you," Marcelle pleaded. "I've never seen a great financier like Coltor close up. I'd love to see what sort of face he has. Faces really interest me, as a painter!"

"I'll take you most gladly, but how?"

"Oh that's not a problem! Tell him I'm your niece, and you didn't want to leave me alone in the hotel."

"True! Wonderful, pure genius!"

"Count," Sandoval intervened, "would it be terribly indiscreet if I asked you to show me this letter?"

"Of course not. Here it is."

He drew it from his pocket and gave it to Sandoval. The painter immersed himself in studying the text. Meanwhile Marcelle called Antas to the other side of the deck to show him something. Sandoval exchanged the letter for another that St Germain had written that morning. It had not been very difficult to concoct a very similar-looking one as the Major had typed his letter on Sandoval's writing paper—a 'chance event' that St Germain was not of course aware of. When the Count returned, Sandoval gave him the second letter, carefully placed back inside the envelope. The Count didn't look inside, but simply stuffed it into his pocket.

They arrived at Burano. When they had seen what there was to see, they sat down to lunch. Antas, as we have already mentioned, would happily drink alcohol whatever the time of day. Now he set about it with gusto. Amorousness and a loyal nostalgia for home induced an even greater thirst in him, and Marcelle and Sandoval did little to discourage him.

"Tell me, Count, are you on good terms with this Coltor?" Marcelle asked.

"On good terms? My dear, I might say that he was frankly eating out of my hand on his last visit to Alturia. We caroused together every night. The only problem was that the poor little chap couldn't hold his liquor. He got drunk immediately and talked total rubbish from then on."

"How interesting. And how did you address each other? Were you on first-name terms?"

"But of course we were," Antas fibbed, seeing how much this seemed to impress Marcelle. "It was always things like 'my dear boy'."

"He called Coltor his 'dear boy'! Did you hear that, Sandoval? Wonderful! And you would just go up to him and pat him on the cheek like that, and say things like 'What ho! my dear boy,' and that sort of thing?"

"But of course. Coltor loved my informal manner, and my eternal good humour."

"But that I can't believe, Count, if you will forgive me. These Norlandians are so dour, and so very reserved, it just isn't possible to talk to them like that," said Sandoval.

"What's that? You don't believe me? And do you believe me, Marcelle?"

"I'm not sure."

"But that's how it was."

"Well, let's see. Let's go to him right now, and you can show us it's true. Pat him on the cheek, and give him the old 'What ho!' then."

"All right. Let's go!" Antas roared, in his drunken overconfidence. "And I'll tell you something else. You think I'm scared of Coltor? What a joke. Me, afraid of a common merchant? I can do what I want with him, whatever I feel like. So there. You'll see."

He was no more sober on the boat going back, and when they got to the Lido Sandoval and Marcelle made doubly sure by getting him to drink two bottles of maraschino before going up to meet Coltor. Sandoval sat in the foyer to await the outcome.

When Antas presented his card to Coltor's secretary, the man spent a moment staring in astonishment at his blurred features and uncertain bearing, but after St Germain's triumphant incursion he simply dared not risk denying immediate entry to any Alturian. He felt sure that any news of that country would now be of even greater interest to his boss.

And so it happened that a few moments later Antas marched into his room, with Marcelle at his side.

Coltor came up to him and bowed politely.

"Hello, my dear boy," Antas bellowed, using the full

power of his lungs, and patting Coltor on the cheek as he stood there stock still in surprise. "So then, what ho, what ho?" was the next bellowed question, accompanied by a knowing sideways glance at Marcelle. "Do you still like those smelly cheeses?"

Coltor was not easily disconcerted, but by now he had almost completely lost his bearings. He threw an enquiring glance at Marcelle, who gave him a conspiratorial look as if to say it was all Antas' doing.

"Well, er … my dear Count … I am delighted to receive … so glad you've come, old pal … "

"I should hope you would be, my dear boy," Antas boomed. "You certainly would if you knew why I've come! Oh yes—and I've brought my little niece with me … " (Coltor bowed to Marcelle) … "who is so splendidly … splendidly charming, and pretty, and clever, and an altogether wonderful young woman … But you only have to look at her, so why I am I telling you this? … So, what do you think of my little niece, my dear boy?"

"But Uncle Ugolino," Marcelle responded modestly, and cast another conspiratorial glance at Coltor.

"Take a seat, Count," said Coltor (by now thoroughly nervous). "Would you like a glass of cold water?"

"Water? For an Antas? What are you thinking of, dear boy?"

"So then, to what do I owe the honour of this visit?"

"To what … ? Wait a sec … I can't think what it was, right now … Oh yes, now I have it. My dear fellow, I have come to save you."

"To save me? Me? From what?"

132

"My poor old Coltor, you are such a trusting little chap you don't even know what danger you are in. My boy, I have words to whisper in your ear. Coltor, you are entangled in a swindlers' net!" he bellowed, inches away from the man's ear.

Coltor leapt back.

"What sort of swindlers are you talking about?"

"Well, that I can't exactly say, because, whaddya call it … you know … because, right now, I'm in love. But take a look, here's the letter, from my good friend Palawer, you'll find it all in there."

And he handed over the letter.

It read:

*Most respected Mr Coltor,*

*I must ask you to make allowances for my unfortunate friend Count Antas. The events of the Alturian Revolution and the abdication of his beloved monarch disturbed him so much that he has not yet managed to regain his mental balance. He suffers from a number of paranoid delusions: there are swindlers everywhere, he is quite convinced there is conspiracy afoot—which is understandable—and he is forever trying to expose it. He has now asked me to write to you since he absolutely insists on talking to you, to reveal yet another great plot. I felt unable to deny his request, but I am sending his niece to keep an eye on him, and perhaps head off any unseemly behaviour. Again I beg you to make allowances for a sadly afflicted man, and to do your best, in all kindness, to steer well clear of him.*

*Till we meet again soon*

*St Germain*

Coltor folded the letter carefully and put it in his pocket. Antas remained seated, and in a trice had nodded off to sleep.

"Is it often like this with the poor chap?" he asked Marcelle quietly.

"Poor Uncle Ugolino, his drinking really is a bit excessive these days … but you can understand why … the grief … "

Antas' head jerked upwards.

"Well, my dear boy," he shouted, if somewhat groggily, "what ho, what ho?"

"My dear Count, I am delighted to have seen you, and I am most sorry that you have to leave, but your kind niece informs me that you have pressing business elsewhere."

"Yes, yes, of course … And the letter? Have you read it?"

"Of course I've read it. And I must thank you very much for bringing it to my attention. I shall be forever in your debt for exposing this plot."

"No need for thanks; what I did … you know … what I did … sacrifice to honour and country … do you follow me?"

"But of course."

"That's good, then. God be with you."

And, supported by Marcelle, he staggered out of the room.

The next morning St Germain gave Sandoval and Marcelle a lively ovation on their arrival at the Palazzo Pietrasanta to hear about his plans.

"Well done, *maestro* Sandoval. You did a marvellous job. I never knew so much talent in a painter. If you ever decide to give up art for another profession I predict a great future for you. But the most important thing we've learnt from all this is that we have to move quickly. Who knows, this Palawer could still bring us down. We can't afford a second's delay. I'd prefer to wait a bit longer but I can see that that's not possible. My dear Sandoval, by the end of today we shall have held a meeting that will resound throughout history."

"By this afternoon? Including the preparations?"

"My people are already here: Baudrieu, Valmier and Gervaisis have arrived. I'll brief them before lunch and they'll see to everything we might need. We're still short of one person. That is to say, Princess Ortrud is to be here in the palace. Marcelle will take the role. Then, along with Marcelle, we need an elderly countess to chaperone her. After all, Princess Ortrud can hardly call in at her fiancé's palazzo, even in incognito."

"This isn't going to be easy," said Sandoval. "First of all, where are we going to get an old countess at short notice? Also, Coltor already knows Marcelle as Antas' niece. Is Ortrud's presence really necessary?"

"At any rate, it's highly desirable. It would persuade Coltor that the King's intentions are serious, that he really does want to return to the throne, he wants to marry her, and he's not going to have second thoughts. The fact that Coltor has already seen Marcelle is immaterial. Marcelle will wear entirely different make-up, and she's a superb actress. As for the old countess ... now, where can I find one of those?"

"Well, where?"

"I have it. St Germain's resourcefulness is inexhaustible. Now, my young friend, can you guess who will be the old countess?"

"I've no idea."

"But it's so simple. Like a crossword puzzle. You will be the old countess."

"Me?"

"Naturally. I'll make you up myself. The sort of wonderfully ugly old countess you might paint in one of your pictures."

"Splendid," said Sandoval, resignedly.

"So, no difficulty there. No difficulty at all. There's only one problem, and that's a rather specific one."

"What's that."

"The leading man. Oscar. Oscar the psychological mystery. Because, whether you think so or not, Oscar is a psychological mystery. A mystery even my rapier brain can't penetrate."

"How do you mean, Count?"

"It's something I can't quite put into words. I just feel— it's my miraculous intuition—that I can never be quite sure of him. You can never be certain he's actually there. He could go off the rails at any moment. It wouldn't surprise me if he just suddenly disappeared. Or at the very last moment, on the field of battle, face to face with Coltor, he might do something completely unexpected. For example, blurt out that he isn't really the king, or that he is the king but he won't sign the treaty. I tell you, he's capable of anything. Ah, but here are the excellent

Baudrieu, and the inimitable Valmier. Allow me to introduce you gentlemen to one another. Baudrieu, you must call on Coltor before lunchtime, and inform him— with all the usual bowings and scrapings—that the hour of decision is upon us, and he must come to the Palazzo Pietrasanta tomorrow afternoon."

"Very good, boss."

"Valmier, here is an Alturian flag. Find a place for it on the wall. There we are. And now hang there, glorious banner, with your two golden sardines on a field of silver, and bring blessings on your sons. Now, Valmier, you must don your time-honoured livery, and apply your celebrated cheek-whiskers. A visitor will be arriving in the next few hours and we need a footman."

"Very good, boss."

"Then why aren't you going?"

"Well, boss, I had to take out the livery from the pawnbroker, and then my travel expenses … if I could trouble you for a little advance … "

"When you are properly dressed, my young friend, I shall give your request consideration … and you, Sandoval, are to undertake any artistic duties we decide on. The toothpaste advertisement is up in the top room. Turn it into a portrait of Philip II or the One-Eared. We must spread a little meaningful Alturian atmosphere around the place."

At that moment Mawiras-Tendal entered, with a bird-cage in his hand.

"Very suitable," said St Germain. "Here we have Dio-genes, His Highness' favourite canary. Things are starting to take shape."

"Where are we going to put it?" the Major asked.

"We'll take it up to the great hall, where the meeting will be held. His Highness doesn't like being without his favourite canary for a single minute. Oh yes, I haven't yet told you, Mr Meyer. I have decided on the time. It's this afternoon."

The Major looked at St Germain in astonishment.

"Why so soon?"

"We can't act quickly enough. There are traitors all around us. Somebody is trying to scupper our little enterprise. He's already tried to expose us. But the miserable fellow forgot that he was dealing with St Germain. My arm has a long reach. I'm not referring to statesmen, of course, but I would venture to assert that there is no private individual in all Europe whose arm has such a long reach. I knew of this shabby little plan, and I put a stop to it with no trouble at all. That's the person I am."

The Major went pale, and put the cage down.

"To the devil with this bird," he said with exasperation. "Does Oscar know it's this afternoon … ?"

"He doesn't know, because I have only just decided. Do go, my dear Meyer, and tell him. He's here in the palazzo somewhere."

There was no need to tell the Major twice; he rushed off immediately. He found Oscar in the room assigned to Marcelle.

"Oscar, I have to talk to you urgently. Alone."

They went out onto the street so that they could speak without fear of being interrupted.

"Your Highness," the Major began.

" 'My dear fellow'," Oscar corrected him.

"Your Highness," the Major repeated, rather more firmly. "We haven't time just now for casual informality."

"What is it, what's happened? Don't make me nervous!"

"Permit me, Your Highness, to make you very nervous. We haven't a second to waste. St Germain has invited Coltor to this damned palazzo this afternoon."

"Hm. He's in such a hurry?"

"Yes. And now we really have no choice but to disappear."

For some time the King maintained a sombre silence. Then he replied:

"Can you think of no other solution, Major? I really would like you to find some other way out. I would feel terrible leaving them in the lurch. St Germain is such a decent chap. A great talent. Without him I would never have known what to do if I were still king. It just proves it—even kings have to get to know life."

"Your Highness, there is no other solution. You simply cannot meet Coltor here. We must leave for Trieste on the twelve o'clock train."

"Yes, yes, I see that. And Marcelle?"

"I'd say yes, we should take her with us, but I'm afraid she would never leave St Germain in the lurch a few hours short of the realisation of his great plan. But we can write to her from Trieste a day or two after we get there and ask her to come. If Your Highness would still wish that … "

" … if I still wished it. You are quite right, I would. But

139

the fact is, if I leave now it'll be the end of everything, signed and sealed; and Marcelle, I am afraid, would no longer be a concern. Well, Milán, I must go and take my leave of her."

"But Your Highness!"

"It's all right, my Milán. I know what you want to say. She won't suspect for a moment that I am saying goodbye. I just want to see her once more. She was very good to me … and this whole business has been very instructive."

The King found Marcelle alone in her room. She had been putting on her Princess Ortrud costume, as they had conceived of it after studying pictures in the newspapers of the way she wore her hair, and how she looked at the time of the revolution. When the King saw her made up like this, he just stood there in the doorway, turned to stone: so strong was the resemblance to Ortrud.

"Your Highness … " she began, and performed a deep curtsey, as St Germain had just taught her.

The King raised his hands in front of him, like a man warding off an apparition.

"Sensational," he stammered.

"Well, how do you like it?" she asked.

He continued to stare in astonishment.

"But, you know, it's perfect. Just perfect."

"Am I beautiful?"

"They're so right for you, the make-up, the dress—you must wear them always."

"What do you think: do I look like her?"

"Until you open your mouth. The moment you speak, the resemblance stops."

"Really?" Suddenly she looked at him in amazement. "You talk as if … you've seen her."

"Y—yes. I was over there once … she was playing tennis."

"So. Is she beautiful?"

"It's a matter of taste."

Some jealous suspicion had stirred in Marcelle, and his confused answers were simply reinforcing it.

"Tell me, Oscar … tell me: would you rather I were really her?"

"You know I love you just as you are."

"What am I 'just as'?"

"For example, as you are now, dressed as Princess Ortrud. That's how I love you."

"How much?" she asked coyly.

"So much," he replied, embracing her and showering her with kisses.

She pulled away, and snapped angrily at him:

"You snake! You lying snob. It isn't me you love, it's the princess!"

The King was horrified. She was absolutely right. The thought of Ortrud had been so strong, and so unexpected. He simply did not understand himself. He had always been too busy to realise how attractive she was, from a distance.

"What are you saying?" he asked, appalled. "Do you really think that?"

"Of course," she replied, and burst into tears. "Oh, Oscar, the moment you saw me in this mascara you looked on me as someone different—someone utterly different.

A woman can tell. You're already bored with me, Oscar! You'd much rather have a real lady! A baroness, or something. You worm!"

"Not in the least," he lied: "not in the least, my angel. You're the only one I love. Don't cry."

He tried to hold her in his arms and console her, but she pushed him away angrily.

"You liar, you liar! You haven't been kissing me. Don't you dare speak to me. I've had enough. You can go to the devil. Go to your baroness."

"Please, Marcelle, this is very important," he said quietly. "I have to explain something to you … "

In truth, he would have loved to explain this double reality to himself, and the whole turmoil of feelings contending inside him.

"No explanations! I know how stupid you are. When a man has to 'explain' it's always been worse than you thought."

"Don't talk so much, my angel. I really must explain. It's true I find you attractive in a different way, in all this make-up, but … "

"Oscar!"

"Don't shout, angel, don't shout, just for a moment. The reason why I find you so attractive is that you aren't a real princess, but, well … because you are Marcelle. That is to say, because you are what you are. How the devil can I put this into words? Look, there are umbrellas that look like sticks, yes?"

"So they say."

"So you see," he said triumphantly. "There are books

that when you open them you find sugar inside, and there are slide rules you can use as thermometers, and there are trouser-braces with compasses in them, so do you now understand?"

"Twaddle!"

"You see, there's nothing more exciting than when you're one person and also someone else … and you see how different the two of them are, and the separate worth of each … "

"What a lot of twaddle you talk, Oscar!"

"Quite right, Marcelle. Why am I talking so much? When all I want to say, is how horribly much I love you."

"So why do you still love me?" she asked, nuzzling up close to him.

"I love you because you are such a straightforward girl, I mean about life," the King said, more to himself than to her. "The other woman, the Princess … would never know how to say 'twaddle', especially not in that dress … Please, say it again: 'twaddle!' "

"Twaddle," she replied, in a voice that wavered, full of love.

"You angel!" At that moment he loved her more than ever. But at the same moment he also loved Ortrud more than ever. It was as if she were the one who had said the word 'twaddle'. It showed her in a completely new light. She was no longer merely the daughter of the Gracious Empress Hermina. She had suddenly acquired the interest, and the mystery, of a woman.

They kissed again.

"Oh, Oscar … if only it were night," she whispered.

"Yes, indeed," he replied. And then a sudden horror seized him. "Holy God ... tonight ... "

"What is it? What's wrong with you?"

"Marcelle, tonight is still a long way away ... so much could happen before then!"

"Such as?"

"Such as ... a serpent rising out of the sea."

"Have you gone mad?"

"Of course not. It's happened a thousand times in the past, in history."

He began kissing her with real passion, filled with grief at the approaching separation.

"Let me go, Oscar—you've completely ruined my princess face. What's the matter with you? You were always such a quiet boy ... "

"I had time to spare then. I always believed that I'd start really loving you the next day. But now ... "

He pulled her close once again, and started to kiss her. Being French, Marcelle liked to talk in moments of passion.

"Oh, Oscar ... I love it, you're like an express train ... like a wild sheikh ... like a bartender at closing time ... "

At just that moment in came Valmier, in full livery and side whiskers.

"Hey!" he said, and went up to the King, who hadn't noticed the arrival in the heat of his ardour.

"That's quite enough, old boy," he observed, and clapped him on the shoulder.

The King spun round, seized him by the throat, then immediately released him.

"I beg your pardon," he said, "harbinger of the sea serpent."

"Tell me, girl," Valmier asked Marcelle: "Does this man pass as normal with you people?"

Then, turning to the King:

"Now, get a move on. Pronto! The boss is calling for you. He wants a word with you right away."

"Coming," the King replied. "So then … tonight, Marcelle."

"Hey, old boy, hang on a sec!" Valmier shouted after him. "Look, you'd better tell St Germain it's not on."

"What do you mean? What's not on?"

"What I said earlier. Just my expenses, my livery, my travel … it'll cost you people at least three hundred lire."

"Three hundred?" Marcelle laughed. "You'll be lucky. There aren't three hundred lire in the whole building."

"I don't care—that's your problem," Valmier said, furiously. "What a bunch of … And this is what I left the old Yank for!"

"Look, Jean," Marcelle replied. "Just be a little patient. Tomorrow, money will be raining down on us. Isn't the name of St Germain good enough, in our line of trade?"

"I've heard of better. I think he's gone a bit senile. Well, old boy, you can tell him that if I don't get my three hundred lire, I quit."

Marcelle began to plead with him.

"Jean, you couldn't leave us in such a fix? Jean—for my sake … !"

"For your sake? Not for yours, or anyone else's. I'm going on strike. This minute."

145

And he ripped off his beard.

"Holy God," Marcelle shouted. "Oscar, talk to the Count!"

"I'll send him up straight away," the King replied, and raced off.

Valmier came up to Marcelle.

"Marcelle, I sent that jerk away so I could ask you: how serious is this thing? Do you really like that puppy?"

Marcelle turned away and replied, almost as if ashamed:

"Well … yes … I do. Why?"

"Rubbish. What do you see in him? He hasn't got a clue about anything. Uselessness is written all over him. The only thing he's good for is a fall guy when the cops arrive."

"Yes, I know. But perhaps that's just why I love him. You know, he is just a little bit soft in the head. He was going on just now about some serpent from the sea."

"Marcelle, this whole thing is just wrong for you."

"I think so, too," she said, sadly. "He's starting to get bored with me."

"So it's obvious. In your place I wouldn't wait for the bloke to dump me."

"And … ?"

"Clear out. Marcelle, this whole thing really isn't making you happy. There's going to be a complete smash-up, and we two'll have the cops round our necks."

"Nonsense. What makes you think so?"

"You don't think anyone with any intelligence will believe this chum of yours is a king? This infant? This

146

half-wit? It's a joke. The moment your mister claps eyes
on this king of yours, the whole thing'll go up in smoke."

"You think so?"

"I'd lay good money on it. And then you'll all be in the
nick."

"My God, and my diamond ring's gone down the
spout."

"I'm telling you, we'd better get out before it's too late.
Marcelle, come with me. I've got this gondolier friend;
he'll take your things to the station."

"And then what do I do with myself?"

"Just leave that to me. In Paris you'll make a pile from
this chipmunk from the States. He runs after women like
a baby."

"And Oscar?"

"To hell with Oscar," Valmier snarled, and drew back.
"Aren't I good enough for you?"

At that moment St Germain came charging in.

"Valmier … get your beard on!" he shouted.

"Well … I haven't got one … " Valmier parried.

"You see how it is, Marcelle my girl," said St Germain
in a trembling voice. "You spend your whole life slaving
away for your friends, and for your noblest ideals; you put
up with the fatigue, the expense, you pour your whole life,
night and day, into your work, so that, just when you get to
the big moment, everything comes crashing down through
the obstructiveness of fools and insignificant layabouts.
Like Alexander the Great at the gates of Paradise."

Deeply moved, Valmier struggled to restore his beard
to its proper place.

"Only three hundred lire, boss," he whined. "Two hundred … "

"And all this for three hundred piddling lire," St Germain thundered. "What are you thinking of? What are three hundred lire to St Germain? A grain of sand on the beach; a single star in the firmament … Marcelle, my dear girl, give this good man fifty lire."

Her eyes bright with tears, Marcelle took off her shoe, extracted fifty lire, and held it out to Valmier.

"There you are."

The Major had been waiting patiently, a Baedeker in his hand, studying the hotels and principal sights of Trieste. Finally the King returned. The Major leapt to his feet.

"So we're off then?"

"So we're not going, my Milán. We're staying."

"But Your Highness!"

"Pardon: 'old fellow'."

"As you wish, Your Highness: but why are we staying?"

"Milán, it's very hard to explain. Whatever else happens, I want to be with Marcelle tonight."

"But Your Royal Highness, Marcelle will be following us to Trieste … or I just don't understand. If you will pardon your most loyal subject, Your Highness was never of such a hot-blooded nature … and women, if I might say so, never influenced your decisions before. So why now?"

"You are right, Milán. You know me well. It's not really about my wanting to spend another night with Marcelle. This is something entirely different. The fact is, if I left now, I'd feel my love for Ortrud so strongly I might do something insane. For all I know, I'm quite capable of taking up the throne again to marry her. And that I really do not want. Only Marcelle can cure me of this madness."

"This is terrible," the Major agreed. "You've never suffered from romantic complications before. But just think, Your Highness, what will happen if we stay. This afternoon you will have to negotiate with Coltor. You will have to act as if you're Oliver VII, former King of Alturia, even though you really are him. How can you get out of such an impossible situation? It makes a man's brain seize up … "

"Trust me, Milán."

"Does Your Highness have a plan?"

"No. Not exactly. But I'll get by somehow. I shall trust to the spur of the moment, and our Alturian talent for conspiracy. I got out of a far more difficult situation: being king."

"But Your Highness, we cannot afford to take risks … "

"Leave it, Major." This was said in an altogether different tone, altogether more aloof.

Hearing it, the Major stiffened to attention and stood staring in undisguised wonder at the King. This commanding presence was not something he was much used to.

"A king's fate can be decided only by a king, Major.

When I need to, I will make the decisions. Thank you, Major."

The Major stood at ease.

"Now let's go and have a well-earned lunch."

St Germain had been right: there are always traitors, everywhere: as many traitors as there are people. Every one of Coltor's secretaries had been hand-picked, not just for ability, but for their loyalty. Nonetheless, among them was a traitor.

The moment this person—whose name is of little importance to our story—knew that Coltor had made contact with Oliver VII, he immediately passed what had happened on to Harry Steel, the world-renowned reporter from the *New York Times*, who happened just then to be in Venice. Steel, who had been the Alturian correspondent at the time of the revolution and had ever since been regarded as America's leading expert on that country, received the news in understandable excitement. He had instantly written the man a substantial dollar cheque, and was now calling him up every hour for further revelations.

But this wasn't enough, and he set off to discover more himself. He looked round the Lido, and wherever people congregate in Venice, hoping to come upon someone or something. He was a man whose industry knew no bounds. This was the reporter who had, on one ill-advised occasion, interviewed a terrified Russian Tsar just minutes after a bomb attack.

His vigilance produced a reward. Although, to his puzzlement and surprise, he failed to find the ex-King, he did come upon Count Antas, sprawling alone on the Lido sands and pining for Marcelle. Steel knew the Count by sight from his Alturian days. Wasting no time, he went quickly across and sat down on the sand beside him.

"I say, Count, there's no denying it. I know everything."

"Did my wife send you?" Antas replied, in mortal terror.

"Among others, Count."

"It's all a pack of lies," he whined. "A person of my standing cannot move without attracting the most appalling suspicion and speculation."

"I must advise you, Count, that I have proof in my possession. Handed to me by the secretary … "

"Secretary?" he gasped. And he thought of Sandoval. Ah, yes, that rascally painter! And this detective—for what else could this American be?—thought that Sandoval was Marcelle's secretary.

"Now listen here, my good friend," he said. "Believe you me, the name Antas isn't just empty air; and, take my word for it, there's nothing between her and me. On my honour."

Steel's smile was benevolent, but sceptical.

"That's what they all say."

"I tell you, my feelings towards the young lady in question are those of a father. It's her creative development that interests me. I want to help her become a great artist."

(This was the usual formula, before the war.)

Harry Steel frowned.

"Don't try to put one over on me, Count. What's this girl you're talking about?"

"What? You don't know who I'm talking about, and yet you have the nerve to come here? You crooked rascal!" he shouted, his self-confidence returning. "Who are you anyway?"

"I am Harry Steel," the reporter declared, and held out his hand. "Correspondent of the *New York Times*."

"Well, I can't say I'm pleased to meet you," Antas replied loftily. He did not offer his hand. "So what were you talking about, then? Whose secretary?"

"Now come on, Count, no use pretending. This isn't diplomacy, it's real life. I'm talking about Coltor's secretary, of course."

Once again Antas turned deathly pale.

"Look, it could just be that the secretary saw us together, when we paid our respects to Mr Coltor. But that really means nothing, nothing at all."

"What? You went there with the King?"

"To hell with the King! What king are you talking about anyway?"

"I wouldn't try putting one over old Harry Steel, Count. I know for a fact that Oliver VII has been negotiating with Coltor. He wants to get back on the throne and sign the treaty."

Antas' sense of mastery returned at once, and he exploded with furious laughter:

"King Oliver negotiating with Coltor? Wonderful. Quite wonderful … Now you can clear off, young man. We Antases like to enjoy the sunshine on our own."

152

"Count, it seems you still don't grasp what I'm talking about, or you wouldn't think it a joke. They're keeping it top secret. But it's your duty to take an interest in what's happening, and you could be of assistance to me … "

"I don't know what you're talking about? I was the one who opened Coltor's eyes to the fact that he had been caught by swindlers."

Steel became highly excited.

"Swindlers? I didn't know that. For God's sake, tell me more, Count. At this moment the whole of America is hanging on your lips."

The image seized Antas' imagination. Half the world dangling from his lips, like a cigarette. He told Steel all he knew, while the reporter listened amazed, in a fever of curiosity. Then he jumped to his feet and said:

"Count, wait here a moment. I'll be right back. Warm your illustrious person in the sun for a moment. It's crucially important that you wait for me."

"Just be quick, young man," Antas replied. "My skin feels as if it's starting to burn."

Steel raced headlong to the nearest telephone booth and rang Coltor's secretary.

"Hello. Steel here. Mr Secretary? Have you heard the great news?"

"Oh yes. Four this afternoon."

"What's at four this afternoon?"

"Letting the canary out."

(This was the name for the negotiations that had been agreed for use over the telephone, to prevent Coltor's entourage knowing of the secretary's betrayal.)

153

"Where?" Steel asked.

"That I can't tell you right now. Come to the hotel right away."

Steel dashed back to the beach, then ploughed his way between the sprawling bathers.

"Count," he puffed, "something doesn't add up. Either they've misled you, or you've misled me. The King is going to negotiate with Coltor this afternoon. There's no question about it. Coltor's secretary told me."

"What?" shouted the Count, as he scrambled to his feet. "It's impossible. Coltor talking to those scoundrels after all that? In spite of my warning?"

"Did you give your warning sufficient emphasis, Count?"

Antas became troubled.

"Well, you know, the constraints of the situation … considering the long-standing intimate friendship between the two of us … it could be that I did express myself in too frivolous a manner; perhaps he was just carried away by my irresistible wit … "

" … and didn't take you seriously?"

"Yes, that's always possible. These Norlandians are such dour people, if you aren't wearing sackcloth and ashes when you tell them something they don't actually believe you. That could be it. How horrible! These swindlers will make Alturia a laughing stock forever!"

"We've no time to lose. We can still expose them, and then all the glory will be ours. What a report that'll make!"

"I am at your service, Mr Editor. What do we have to do?"

"First of all, get your clothes on. Then be so good as to come to my hotel. You'll get the rest of your instructions there."

When the King and the Major returned after lunch to the Palazzo Pietrasanta, preparations had reached fever pitch.

A revoltingly ugly old woman was darting back and forth with surprising energy.

St Germain introduced her: "The Plantagenet Duchess. She's a little deaf."

"A little deaf, but very ugly," the King observed.

"Not so fast! I heard that," said the Duchess, alias Sandoval.

Honoré arrived from Sandoval's upstairs studio, brandishing a large picture.

"Is the ladder here?" St Germain asked. "Now you need to hang it. I'll tell you where in a moment."

All expertise, he paced up and down the room, then pointed to a spot on the wall.

"We'll put it there. It'll be seen to best advantage there."

Honoré nailed the picture to the wall.

"Who is this monster?" the King asked. "Why is he leering at me like that, and why has he got a tooth mug in his hand?"

"It's the toothpaste advert. We repainted it," said St Germain. "It was originally a king brushing his teeth, now it's Philip II or the One-Eared, a former King of Alturia. You can recognise him from his enormous ear, a triumph of artistic skill by our friend Sandoval. Oscar, you should have learnt more Alturian history. I've told you enough about it."

"But why is he grinning like that?" the King asked.

"Because in the advertisement there was a toothbrush in his hand. But I took it out," Sandoval explained modestly.

"The canary, Honoré," commanded St Germain.

Honoré had already brought it.

"Diogenes, His Highness' favourite canary. It conjures up a bit of cosy Alturian atmosphere."

Valmier entered, the perfect footman.

"Here's the jewellery, boss."

"Indeed? I'll go and sort it out and have the necklace made up—the one Princess Ortrud is to have as a gift from the King. Oscar, time to robe up."

"Me? What in?"

"The marshal's greatcoat of course. I've already told you, young man, it's a sacred tradition. He never appears in public without his marshal's greatcoat on. It's up in the studio. Sandoval will be so kind as to show you how to put it on and wear it. Off you go, young man."

Off he went, at speed.

"The greatcoat?" he sighed. "My Milán," he whispered: "is this what the revolution was for?"

In the room next door he stumbled over a gentleman sleeping in the depths of an armchair with his legs splayed out.

"Who's that?" he asked.

"That's one of the Count's great discoveries," Sandoval answered. "Gervaisis, the eternal sleeper."

"Wake him," said the King.

Sandoval shook the man.

"Hey, mister, wake up."

The sleeper came to and spoke:

"Who sows the wind will reap the whirlwind."

"Excuse me?" the King replied.

"Nothing," Gervaisis remarked. "Just an old proverb. I always say one when I wake up."

"Congratulations."

"Thank you," he retorted, and went back to sleep.

"St Germain brought him here because he thinks his aristocratic somnolence will raise the tone of the meeting."

"I've also been wondering about the tone," the King observed.

They arrived at the studio. Even with the assistance of two helpers the King had great difficulty getting the coat on. It was rather more extravagant and ornate than the original.

"Do I have to?" he asked. "Compared to this, the one at home was a housecoat."

"Your Highness," the Major implored him. "You can still reconsider!"

"How can you think that, Milán? Now that I've come this far, and actually got inside this damn thing? I'm not going to take it off now. You'd better get your major's uniform on. It's over there, on the bed. You'll see what a strange feeling it is, meeting it again."

157

By the time they returned to the hall, everyone was assembled. Honoré was strutting proudly up and down in his military costume; the eminent pseudo-lawyer Baudrieu, in a green jacket, was seated at the negotiation table, with its covering of green baize, putting his papers in order. Gervaisis was deep in an armchair, asleep. Suddenly he gave a loud snort.

"Thank you for bringing that to my attention, Gervaisis," St Germain remarked. "It had quite slipped my mind."

He drew a military decoration from his pocket and stuck it on Baudrieu.

Marcelle appeared, in her full Ortrud costume. It was very restrained. The train was as long as a barge.

"Let's have a look at you, my girl," the Count said. "Allow me to apply the final strokes of the brush. Stand over there, so we can see you better. Honoré, give me that illustrated newspaper."

He jerked his head back, closed one eye, and compared Marcelle with the photograph.

"Perhaps the eyebrows a quarter of a centimetre higher, the mouth just a shade smaller … the nose is fine … the *coiffure* excellent. Very good, my girl. Your manner must be friendly but at the same time a little aloof, and don't flirt with Coltor—that might lead to complications—besides, a princess doesn't do that sort of thing. You will greet him with the rest of us, but must leave before we sit down to discussions. When I say to Coltor, 'We never doubted it for a moment,' you must rise and invite the gentlemen to join you upstairs later for a cup of tea, and you can leave the room, attended by our Sandoval."

Gervaisis gave another of his snorts.

"Quite right, Gervaisis," said the Count. "This Gervaisis is an invaluable colleague. I almost forgot to say to you gentlemen that in Alturia people greet each other with 'blessed be the memory of your grandfather'."

The three Alturians exchanged a look.

"Is that right?" the Major asked. "They certainly did in the middle ages, but not now."

"How's that?"

"They say things like 'good morning' or 'your humble servant'."

"Mr Meyer, you share your countrymen's habit of always knowing better than everyone else. But I understand, from very reliable sources, that this is how they greet one another. I read it in a Sunday newspaper. So would you all kindly stick to it."

Marcelle drew the King aside.

"Oscar, you look so beautiful in that costume!"

"You too, my girl, you too," he replied absent-mindedly. Then a thought suddenly struck him. It occurred to him how, in a very similar situation, he had said exactly the same thing to Princess Ortrud. What was happening? Was it becoming so difficult to distinguish between them?

"You should always go about dressed like that," she added.

"Would you want me to? Well, take a good look then, Marcelle. Who knows when you'll have another chance to see me in this coat."

Coltor stepped into the motorboat, with his two secretaries in tow. He was unusually nervous and talkative.

"If this comes off, it'll be the biggest deal of my life," he remarked thoughtfully. "It'll be difficult; very difficult. I never had a deal collapse so very late in the day as that one did when the Alturian revolution broke out. I must say, the thing didn't completely surprise me. That morning, after I'd left my house and was going to my office in the car, a huge black cat ran across the road in front of me. I knew at once it would mean trouble."

The secretaries exchanged glances. His profound superstition was a shared joke between them.

"But the situation is quite different today. When I left my hotel this morning another black cat ran across the road. But immediately a second cat appeared, a tabby. It boxed its ears, and chased it away. So I am quite sure that we'll have better luck today … unless I'm speaking too soon."

That thought thoroughly alarmed him and plunged him into a restless silence.

They arrived alongside the Palazzo Pietrasanta.

"You see, gentlemen," he declared, "the sort of place a real grandee lives in. From a distance the palace may not look much. There's nothing ostentatious. The only adornment is its noble simplicity, and venerable age."

At the entrance they were received by Valmier in a wonderful porter's fur coat and hat; then a uniformed Honoré led them quickly through the main gate into the great hall, where St Germain, Baudrieu and Gervaisis were waiting.

"May the memory of your grandfather be blessed," they shouted in chorus, as Coltor entered.

"I beg your pardon?" he asked in surprise.

"The usual Alturian greeting," St Germain explained.

"That's interesting," Coltor replied. "I never noticed before. No matter."

"First, let me introduce you to Monsieur Baudrieu. Monsieur Baudrieu is an expert on international law—renowned throughout Europe—who has travelled here to assist our negotiations. Next to him is the Marquis of Gervaisis, Grand Master of the Order of St Jacob."

"I knew your dear father," Gervaisis remarked to Coltor. Coltor was taken aback. No one on the entire planet had ever known his father: including himself.

"Would you gentlemen kindly take a seat while we inform His Highness and Princess Ortrud that you have arrived?"

Marcelle, as Ortrud, attended by Sandoval as the Plantagenet Duchess, made her entrance into the room, and Coltor stepped forward to kiss their hands. St Germain explained that the Princess was maintaining absolute incognito while in Venice.

"The poor things," he said in a low voice. "They so much wanted to see each other, and the Gracious Empress Hermina could no longer bear to witness her daughter's unhappiness. Even on royal thrones the hearts that beat are human. But His Highness couldn't go to Norlandia. It would instantly have become general knowledge and given rise to speculation. Geront I, the present ruler of Alturia, would certainly have condemned it. So that is

161

why they met here, in a neutral country and in the sort of place where you can easily lose yourself in the crowd. So far no one has penetrated His Highness' incognito, apart from your own sharp-eyed self."

"Interesting," said Coltor. "In all my life in Norlandia I never heard of the Plantagenet Duchess."

"Oh, it's the collateral line, now quite terminal. But very high-ranking."

"His Royal Highness King Oliver VII," announced Valmier, banging his staff three times on the floor.

The King and his *aide-de-camp* made their entrance. Oliver greeted Coltor warmly.

"Mr Coltor, punctual as ever."

"Punctuality is the courtesy of Captains of Industry," St Germain observed.

A polite conversation ensued, and Coltor assured the King that his incognito, like that of Princess Ortrud, would be treated with the greatest respect.

"Then you would maintain silence even if our discussions happened not to produce the desired result?" the King asked.

"Even then, naturally."

"Mr Coltor, we never doubted it for a moment," St Germain said in a raised voice.

Marcelle took her cue and made her withdrawal speech:

"My dear Mr Coltor, I would not wish to intrude on your important discussions. I shall return to my rooms on the next floor. I hope you will take a cup of tea with us after your meeting."

Coltor thanked her for the invitation, and she and

Sandoval left. At St Germain's behest the others seated themselves round the green table, Baudrieu made a show of spreading out his papers, and Gervaisis immediately fell asleep. Then St Germain called on Coltor to outline his proposals.

"I trust," Coltor began, "we can come to an agreement very swiftly, since there are in effect no grounds of difference between us."

"Indeed not," said Honoré, helpfully.

"It is altogether a question," Coltor continued, "of the original agreement automatically remaining in force, to take effect as soon as His Highness declares his firm intention to return to his ancestral throne and marry Princess Ortrud, which should be considered a *sine qua non* from the Norlandian side."

"But my dear Coltor," the King interrupted with a smile. "That doesn't depend on me alone."

"I thought Princess Ortrud … "

"I'm not thinking of Princess Ortrud, but of my regaining the throne of Alturia … "

"Oh, excuse me," Coltor replied, and now he too smiled, with an airy wave of the hand. "That's something you must be so good as to leave to us. The present ruler sees his position simply as a burden. He would give it all up quite happily in return for a few interesting pictures. Princess Clodia will receive appropriate compensation in Norlandia. She'll be given the Governor-Generalship of a colony somewhat larger than Alturia."

"To live among the natives?"

"Yes."

"That'll suit her. She'll be able to express her manly energy to the full. But Parliament? Government? The people?"

"You must simply leave that to us. I can supply details if you wish. But first, the most important thing is that we come to an agreement in principle."

"Indeed," the King replied, in a low, solemn voice. "I am extremely sorry, my dear Mr Coltor, that we have dragged you here. I am compelled to state here and now that I have no intention of coming to terms with you."

Baudrieu and Honoré, who had been growing increasingly worried that Oscar was doing so much of the talking, now turned pale and glanced at their leader, as did the astonished Coltor. But the Count, with the greatest of composure, declared:

" … His Highness means that he has no intention of agreeing before we have subjected the treaty to considerable revision." He paused to stroke his chin, appeared to be lost for a moment in thought, then continued:

"The treaty in its present form does not address the interests of the poorest class of the Alturian people."

"Hear, hear!" slipped out involuntarily from the Major's mouth. Now it was the King's turn to stare at St Germain in amazement. He had not expected this.

"Alturia, most respected sir," St Germain went on, "is from the social point of view a regrettably backward country. That is why it is His Highness' greatest wish that the Concern, should it win the monopoly in question, would be required to assume a large burden of responsibility for social welfare in Alturia; at its own expense, that is."

"Yes indeed," said the King, looking at St Germain less in astonishment than with a kind of intense joy. Then he himself continued:

"Now listen, Mr Coltor. I have given this matter a great deal of thought ever since. The fishermen and the wine producers will need exemption from all taxes for a period of five years, and the Concern will have to compensate the Treasury for the shortfall. Then, we have to agree the terms on which the fishermen and the wine producers can take out interest-free loans to improve equipment used in production … "

The King paused for reflection, whereupon St Germain took over again:

" … and there are five or six other such desiderata, on which His Highness and his entourage in exile have been working, day and night—at a time, I might add, when everyone thought he was simply spending the time in pleasure pursuits—proposals which we are ready to make available to Mr Coltor for his consideration over the next few days, should Mr Coltor indicate his willingness in principle to meet these demands."

Coltor did not answer. He was thinking, and seemed to be calculating. But it had clearly struck him what a huge opportunity it all meant, even if the treaty came into being subject to these stipulations. He replied:

"Very good. This is something we can discuss. I am in the happy position of being able to make certain concessions."

"We thank Mr Coltor in advance, and most warmly, for these concessions," said the King. "But this is still minor; very minor."

"Hear, hear," chimed Baudrieu and Honoré. They had been thinking they were going to get nothing from this wonderful outcome.

"Your Highness is clearly thinking," said St Germain, "that it is hardly possible either to win your country back, or to govern it, without money, and our little royal household in the course of our residence abroad … "

"Forgive me, my dear Chief Courtier, but that is not among my concerns. There are matters at stake here of far greater importance than questions of money. For example, that the treaty, without reservation or pre-condition, must be subordinate to the principle of national self-determination. It might be beneficial from the economic point of view, but from the moral standpoint, and that of national pride, it is impossible. An ancestral kingdom, a living monarchy, cannot be made the plaything of a stockmarket company. You would need to amend the treaty to allow for a regular monitoring body, composed of Alturian statesmen and representatives of the people, to exercise a veto should the Concern exceed its powers, and to be responsible for its general working to the Alturian Parliament."

"Hear, hear," the Major chipped in now.

"I find it a little strange," said Coltor, "that we have talked so much about the people and their rights. This is a matter for His Highness on the one hand, and the Concern on the other. In my opinion, the people are a secondary consideration."

The King raised his voice:

"Mr Coltor, you are wrong. Profoundly wrong. They are the primary consideration. If you really want to know … that's why … "

He was going to say, "why I didn't hold on to the crown. Because I did not know how to help myself, and I had no wish to sell my people into servitude; and, caught between two impossible situations, I chose a third and ran away".

But instead he remained silent. St Germain had meanwhile intervened:

" … and that is why, recognising His Highness' generous and benevolent nature, we have proposed these amendments."

"Excuse me," said Coltor, "this insistence on a monitoring body raises one or two difficulties. You cannot subject the accounts and general running of a business enterprise to political control. Business is business, Your Highness, and I can't have people poking their noses in. If people had ever stuck their noses into my companies I wouldn't be the Coltor I am today. I'd be a greengrocer in one of the smaller towns in Norlandia."

"Of that I have no doubt," the King retorted. "But I am obliged to state, with the greatest possible emphasis, that I absolutely insist on such control in all circumstances."

"In that case would you kindly allow me a few days to consider the matter, while we move on to discuss the other details?"

"The most I can allow you for reflection is fifteen minutes. Until you accept my terms, I have nothing more to discuss."

"Of course we can only indulge His Highness if ... "
St Germain began, in his smoothly insidious way. But the
King interposed sharply:

"Count, you will refrain from interrupting."

St Germain lapsed into silent astonishment.

"I am not in the habit of having my words cut short. I
am doing the talking now."

He spoke in a quiet, determined voice, standing with
one hand resting on the table, in the pose of Louis XIV.

"Splendid!" St Germain whispered to Mawiras-Tendal.
"A king to the manner born!"

"I now suspend this meeting. I shall withdraw with my
*aide-de-camp*, to give Mr Coltor time to consider. Count St
Germain, you will be so good as to inform me when he
has come to his decision."

With that he strode rapidly and resolutely out of the
hall, with Mawiras-Tendal following in his wake.

"So, what do you make of that, my Milán?" he asked,
once they had reached one of the more distant rooms and
sat down. "What have you to say about these surprising
developments?"

"Say, Your Highness? I am barely capable of speech. I
didn't understand a word of any of it."

"I told you I would trust to the spur of the moment.
At first I just wanted to get rid of Coltor. But when St
Germain began to suggest we should do something for
the Alturian poor, it suddenly hit me: now was my chance
to lay down conditions that Coltor could never accept. So
I was able to rescue the situation without having to expose
St Germain's people. The only thing I don't understand,

is what put it into St Germain's head to start talking about the poor—the very people, of course, who should have been the focus of discussion from the outset—the people my own ministers back home never even thought worth considering."

"It was clearly St Germain's mysterious ancestor talking to him through the mist of time. But the same mysterious ancestor has now thoroughly wrecked the whole deal. So what will become of us now? If Coltor goes home after this, St Germain's people will beat us to death on the spot."

"No they won't. I'll compensate them. I'll swear we aren't con-men, we really are Brazilian planters. I've got plenty of money and I'll offer them a large sum. On one condition: that they keep it a secret from Marcelle that they got the money from me, so she can go on believing that I am just poor pathetic Oscar. St Germain will come up with some story or other."

"Wonderful, truly wonderful!" the Major growled. "There's just one problem. What will Your Highness do if Coltor actually agrees to set up this monitoring body? If he did, the amended treaty would be better than any you could ever have dreamed of."

"Don't worry, my Milán. Coltor won't agree. If it were simply a question of money he might, because his funds are limitless. But he can't give way on a matter of principle. He wouldn't be Coltor if he had let people stick their noses into his business affairs."

When the King left the meeting Coltor had also withdrawn with his secretaries, to pace up and down in another room and think things over. St Germain remained behind, with his team.

"So what was all that?" Baudrieu asked. "Has Oscar struck out on his own, or has he gone mad?"

"Of course not, my dear friend, of course not," St Germain replied. "It's all part of the game. But, in terms of the agenda, you could say everything's right on course."

"But what was the point of it all?" Honoré asked, anxiously. "All this *spiel* about the poor, and all those other nonentities, instead of talking about what we're going to get? I don't understand any of it."

"There are a great many things you don't understand, my young friend. You can't sign up just like that to a treaty that will decide the fate of an entire people. You have to give things their proper appearance. It's much more realistic if we haggle. And you have to admit, Oscar's acting was sensational. You would really have thought … Anyway, it'll be time to talk about the dough in just a few minutes."

Coltor returned to the negotiation room, treading nervously. The opening of the door woke Gervaisis, who declared:

"Where there is love there is peace."

Coltor stared at him in astonishment.

"Yes indeed, Marquis, my thoughts exactly. We must come to a peaceful agreement. If His Highness is so very determined to have this monitoring body, well then, we'll set one up. I'd like to see the body of men that could monitor me."

"Hear hear," Honoré chimed.

"Most respected sir," said St Germain, "permit me, before we resume our discussions, to take advantage of His Highness' absence to dispose of the sort of questions it might be a little delicate to discuss in his presence."

"Please go ahead, Count."

"The principles of gallantry require His Highness to surprise his fiancée with a gift of some value, from this happy reversal of his fortunes. But our royal household finds itself, temporarily, not in a position ... we have spent months abroad, living in a manner appropriate to his Highness' station ... "

"Naturally, of course, Count. Say no more ... "

And he promptly produced his cheque book.

"I have taken the liberty of choosing this little pendant," St Germain continued, and from his pocket drew the sample of merchandise that the jeweller had just brought round. "Fifty thousand lire the lot, a wonderful bargain ... "

"Fifty thousand? Not worth mentioning, Count, not worth mentioning." And he immediately filled out a cheque for the sum and handed it over.

"Thank you very much," said St Germain, "on behalf of His Highness. We shall of course make this good as soon as the treaty takes effect. And now, I think, there is no bar to our asking His Highness to continue the discussion."

"Come on, you," Honoré called to the King and the Major. "Coltor has accepted your conditions, or whatever that nonsense was about. You must close the deal quickly. I don't understand why you jabbered so much."

"He's accepted?" the Major asked, dumbfounded. "He'll have to be patient for a few more moments."

"Just get a move on," Honoré replied, and went out.

The Major leapt to his feet.

"Your Highness," he shouted. "Your Highness, Coltor has agreed to everything we want. This treaty will ensure Alturia's happiness for a long time to come … if … if … Your Highness would accept it. But of course you can't, because then you'd have to go back to your ancestral throne, and you really don't want that, and so you can't agree to it, because Your Highness is no longer Your Highness but simple Oscar, a common fraudster, and a fraudster can't save Alturia. Though history tells us that Your Highness would not be the first such person to save a nation. So what do we do now, Your Highness?"

"My Milán, right now I just don't know. But let's get back to the negotiation room anyway. We can't stay here."

On their return a new surprise awaited them.

No sooner had Honoré gone to fetch them than a loud commotion was heard outside the negotiation room, voices apparently raised in violent argument. Baudrieu rushed to the door. Gervaisis woke up, and declared:

"No use crying over spilt milk."

The door opened and Valmier and Harry Steel came tumbling in, clinging to each other's hair, while Steel spasmodically grabbed at Valmier's side-whiskers with his free hand. Antas came in hard behind them.

"Boss, this bloke … " Valmier stammered.

"What sort of rascally invasion is this?" St Germain shouted at the intruders. "Gentlemen, I order you to leave. Clear out this minute!"

Harry Steel let go of Valmier and turned to St Germain with a face of gloating triumph.

"So, it's St Germain! I should have guessed you'd have a hand in this."

Then he turned to Coltor and solemnly intoned:

"Mr Coltor, if you are not yet aware of the fact, you have fallen into the clutches of St Germain, the most brilliant swindler of our time. Everything you see here is a deception. This palazzo is not a palace, and these people are not followers of Oliver VII … "

"Holy God," exclaimed Coltor, pointing at Philip II or the One-Eared. The snarl certainly was rather more fierce than usual. "That picture on the wall looked suspicious to me from the start."

"I had my suspicions about the *aide-de-camp*," the first secretary confided.

"What sort of game were they trying on you?" Harry Steel enquired. "I hope to God, Mr Coltor, you haven't yet put any money in their hands?"

"And who are you?" St Germain snapped at Steel. "How dare you come bursting in here! And who is this other specimen you've brought with you?"

"I am Harry Steel, of the *New York Times*; as the Count knows perfectly well."

"And I am Count St Germain, Royal Chief Steward to His Highness King Oliver VII."

"Delighted to meet you," Antas declared. "The Royal Chief Steward is of course none other than myself, Count Antas."

For the first time St Germain seemed a little confused. Coltor glared ominously from one chief steward to the other. At that precise moment, Marcelle entered. She had heard the commotion from the upper floor and raced down, with Sandoval close behind.

"What's going on here?" she demanded. Seeing Antas and Harry Steel, she clapped her hands to her face in horror. "My God! Harry Steel!" She knew him well from a previous incarnation in Paris.

"You see," Valmier hissed into her ear, through his side-whiskers. "I told you we should clear out before it got too late."

"And here's Marcelle," Steel crowed. "St Germain's right-hand woman."

"What?" exclaimed Antas. "She too?"

And his heart broke.

"Mademoiselle, I am delighted to see you," Steel pronounced in his haughtiest tones. "After this, we can have no more pressing duty than to telephone the police."

In an instant Valmier was out through the door and had vanished from the scene of our little history. Marcelle screamed and tried to dash out to alert Oscar to the catastrophe, but Steel blocked her way.

"No one must leave the room!" He seized Marcelle by the arm. "Especially not you. You're staying right here."

She screamed again. At that precise moment the King and the Major appeared. (Honoré, hearing the commotion from outside the room, thought it better to stay there and wait to see what happened.)

In those first moments the only detail of the whole tumultuous scene that caught the King's eye was that someone was holding Marcelle by force. He leapt across, seized Steel by the shoulder and shook him.

"Let her go at once!" he shouted. "Who the hell are you?"

"I am Steel, of the *New York Times*," the journalist declared, taking up the pose of a boxer. "And who the hell are you?"

"I am, er … " the King stammered … but at that moment Antas recognised him, stepped between the two, and greeted his former ruler with a deep bow.

"Your Highness … "

"What's this?" Steel croaked. "Who's a king here?"

"You don't recognise His Royal Highness, King Oliver VII?" Antas asked.

"Oliver VII? The one with the moustache and sideburns … last seen in Kansas City, in his shirtsleeves … "

"I am so happy to see you again, Your Highness," Antas gushed.

"You are welcome, my dear Antas," the King replied graciously, and held out his hand. Then Antas and the Major greeted each other warmly.

Baudrieu rose, and held his hands up to the sky.

"A miracle has happened! There's been nothing like this since the wedding feast at Canaa … "

175

Gervaisis woke up and declared:

"*Autres pays, autres mœurs.*"

Coltor got up and made for the door. He had now lost the thread completely, having gathered just enough of the chaotic situation to make him want nothing more than to get out of this madhouse. The appearance of Antas had done little to reassure him. He had begun to suspect either that everyone present was drunk or that he had been suddenly struck down by some dire affliction.

But Harry Steel stood in his way, and seized his hand with great gusto. Coltor struggled in vain to free it.

"Sensational, sensational!" Steel roared. "I congratulate you, Mr Coltor! No doubt about it—once you get something into your head you should do it! This is great!"

Then he let go of Coltor's hand and turned to St Germain.

"The only thing I don't understand is how you got here."

"So, do you recognise my excellent Chief Steward now?" the King asked, having finally grasped the situation and wanting to rescue St Germain and his friends.

"Your Highness' Chief Steward? But that's me!" Antas wailed.

"Count St Germain has been serving in your stead while we have been abroad, my dear Antas."

"Now I get it!" Steel yelled, in relief. Then he rushed over to St Germain and shook hands with him. "I do beg your pardon, Count. Very foolish of me."

"Not at all, young man, not at all," the Count replied.

"Well then, I must make a call straight away," Steel shouted excitedly, and flew to the telephone.

"Now … " whispered Baudrieu, seizing St Germain's arm. "Now's our chance to clear out. Valmier's already scarpered. Quick, quick. Gervaisis, can you wake up?"

"Of course we're not clearing out, you ox!" St Germain hissed. "We've won!"

"Hello!" Steel boomed into the telephone. "*New York Times*? Steel here. Take a note, please; this is urgent!" Then he went on, in the voice of one dictating: " 'Unexpected developments in the Alturian situation. This afternoon, in Venice's historically renowned Palazzo Pietrasanta, former King of Alturia Oliver VII sat down to negotiate with Mr Coltor, head of the Coltor Concern. According to unofficial sources, their agreement will take effect from today. The King, who is in vigorous health, dropped his incognito and greeted Coltor in his traditional field marshal's greatcoat.' Please transmit this immediately," he concluded, and put the receiver down.

"What happens now?" asked the Major. He was deathly pale. "This is madness. I knew it would all end badly. This Steel has wrecked everything. Tomorrow the whole world will be talking about nothing else. Show us how you'll get out of that, Your Highness."

"Not at all, my Milán, not at all. This pipsqueak American has turned the agreement into a fait accompli. Tomorrow the whole world will know, and we'll have to honour it. No harm in that. What has happened has happened, and perhaps it's better this way. Milán, there have been wise kings who led their countries to disaster, and foolish kings who saved their countries from ruin. Mr Coltor, I must ask you: are you prepared to accept this treaty in the form we began to outline this afternoon?"

"Pardon me. Your Highness needs first to make clear if you are prepared to return to your throne, or whether this whole business has simply been a bit of foolery and confidence trickery."

"I am happy to return to the throne if you will amend your treaty."

"And I am happy to modify my treaty, provided you return."

"Well then ... then, St Germain, you have rescued Alturia. You have brought a treaty into being which I can conclude without shame, and ensured the happiness of my people. But ... " (this was done very quietly) " ... before that, you rescued me. You taught me what it is to be a king."

The King, the Major, Coltor and Antas remained together for a long time, discussing ways of countering any diplomatic contention that might arise between Norlandia and the present government of Alturia as a result of Steel's indiscretion. While this was going on St Germain entertained Steel, who hung on his every word with rapt attention. He knew that not a jot of it was true, but his reporter's heart delighted in this revelation of the Count's ingenuity.

When Coltor's party finally left, thoroughly contented, the King went upstairs to look for Marcelle. But he found only Sandoval, pacing back and forth in agitation. Sandoval was faced with a dilemma. He could not decide whether to keep faith with Princess Clodia or to throw his lot in with the past and present King, to whom, as the Nameless Captain, he had sworn an oath of loyalty. He felt obliged to stand with the weaker party—but he could not make up his mind which of the two was at that moment the weaker.

Almost as if he knew what was passing through Sandoval's mind, the King addressed him:

"Sandoval, I'm going back to Alturia. It's no use. I see now that a king's place is on the throne. Duty isn't a bed of roses. When I came here I was desperate to live the same sort of life as everyone else; to be like an ordinary person. Now I know it's impossible. A man, using the word in its highest sense, has a responsibility, a calling. A fisherman has no vocation to be a king. He'd make a bad king, and the king a poor fisherman. That was my error. We need fishermen, and we need kings. You, my dear Sandoval, stood by me when you stood by the Nameless Captain before you knew who he was, and you stood by me as Oscar the con-man, here, in Venice. Now you must stand beside me in my most difficult hour, when I become King again. Help me take back my throne."

Deeply moved, Sandoval bowed. His decision was made.

"Thank you," said the King. "I have gained my first follower. And now," (in quite a different tone), "do please tell me where Marcelle is."

"Marcelle? She's gone."

"Where to?"

"She didn't say. She just cried and cried, and left this letter for you."

He handed over the envelope. The King opened it. The letter read:

*Your Highness,*
  *Please forgive me. I solemnly take back everything I said. Your Highness is not 'talentless'. Your Highness took me in completely. Your Highness is the most perfect con-man I ever met. Because Your Highness is a truly Royal Highness.*
                                                          *Marcelle.*

King Oliver entered his capital amid general rejoicing. The streets were a-flutter with flags; the Westros department store was adorned with huge portraits of Oliver and Princess Ortrud, seemingly made from entire rolls of silk and broadcloth; mothers held their children up to catch a glimpse of the happily waving King, and loyal inscriptions such as *King Oliver—King of our Hearts*, and *We cannot live without Oliver. Long live the Great Triumphal Return!* were daubed on walls.

King Oliver appeared on the balcony of the royal palace, and greeted his people with a few warm, informal words. The welcome ovation went on forever. Then, when he left the balcony and returned to the room, his government ministers swarmed around to congratulate him.

"Life has taught me a great deal," he told his closest followers. "You can't escape the fact that a man sees things very differently once he has viewed them from below. Clodia, my dear, you should get to know what life is really like."

"No good would come of that!" she replied, deeply offended. "Life is for servants. Let them do it for me."

"Cheep cheep," Count Antas warbled at Diogenes. The King's favourite canary's cage stood beside his writing desk. "Your Highness should have seen how the poor thing pined night and day for his master!"

"But I brought him his hemp seed every day," cooed the fire-eating Delorme.

Gradually the ministers withdrew from the room, revealing Gervaisis deep asleep in an armchair. The newly appointed Colonel Mawiras-Tendal went over and shook him. He woke, and declared:

"Who once puts his hand to the plough should never look back!"

"Quite right," said the Colonel, and led him away.

By now the only people left in the room were the King and Count St Germain, whom the King had asked to stay behind. He offered him a chair and took a seat himself.

"My dear Count," he began, "I kept you here because I want to thank you at this time of happy celebration … "

"No thanks are necessary, Your Highness, none at all."

"I have a great deal to thank you for. I have honoured you with the Grand Cross of the Order of St Florian and appointed you as my financial adviser, but this is truly a small reward for the services you have done me. It was from you that I learnt how to come to terms with the fact that I am a king."

"Well, Your Highness, there are more painful and difficult professions to master."

"There's only one thing I don't understand. You know everything in advance, you plan with enormous care, and what you don't know you seem to sense intuitively ... so is it possible that I, a talentless beginner, could really have fooled you, the master, for so long?"

"We all have our moments of mental blindness. But in fact Your Highness shouldn't be so modest: you played the part of simple Oscar brilliantly. The first time I ever saw Your Highness ... perhaps the voice of my illustrious ancestor whispered to me through the mist of centuries: 'Oubalde Hippolyte Théramene, this gentleman has royal blood!' And I was right to trust him, because he really was an expert on royalty. But then, the message came down through the mist of ages, and perhaps I misunderstood it. Or again, when the illustrious Coltor first recognised Your Highness, it might have occurred to me that a man like that doesn't often get things wrong ... and your reaction could well have given you away to me ... though at moments like that the gods can inflict blindness on the ablest mortal minds. And of course, during the negotiation, even the simplest person, if not actually drunk, must have seen at once that Your Highness was a king, and bore yourself like one ... But perhaps it is more romantic if we content ourselves with the thought that on this one occasion St Germain was taken in. For the first time in my life, and I'm confident it'll be the last. There must surely have been a divine purpose at work here."

"Now I am completely confused. Did I fool you, or did you see through everything?"

"I beg you, Your Highness, not to pursue this. Permit me instead to conduct a little official business."

He stood up and, with the sort of flourish a magician might employ, conjured some jewellery from one of his pockets.

"Your Highness, this necklace was created for you by that jeweller in Venice. It is a gift—something we planned in the Palazzo Pietrasanta of blessed memory. It all went very smoothly, and Mr Coltor has already settled the bill for it. But I must also mention that he gave us a hundred thousand dollars on behalf of the Concern, which we asked for at the time as an advance. He has now made it my reward for services in connection with the treaty."

"Well, well, well. So now we don't have to nip off to Mexico."

"I think this is the most appropriate moment to hand the necklace over to you, as Princess Ortrud will be arriving in Lara within the week."

The King took the necklace and studied it thoughtfully.

"Very beautiful," he said. "Very beautiful, wonderfully executed. But … " (he drew it closer to him, deep in thought) " … properly speaking, it belongs to Marcelle. That ring of hers that we commandeered to hire the Palazzo Pietrasanta, and so laid the foundations of Alturia's prosperity, will not glitter in the pages of history. All the rich people have had a reward. She's the only one who hasn't. How could we possibly forget her? Please, send this little gift to Mlle Marcelle Desbois. I'm sure you'll know where to find her."

"An excellent suggestion, I am sure. But there isn't very far to go. Marcelle is here in the palace."

"What? Here, in the palace?" the King shouted. "And you tell me only now?"

"I thought Your Highness might wish to take your leave of her, and that it might be instructive for you to take one last look … at life, as it is lived down there. If you would be so gracious as to allow me, I shall call her straight away."

A moment later he was back, leading Marcelle by the hand.

"Mademoiselle Marcelle Desbois!" he announced ceremonially.

Marcelle was dressed simply, but very elegantly, for a journey. Her face wore hardly any make-up. She looked at the King with a serious, formal expression, and curtsied.

The King's face lit up, and was again the face of simple Oscar. It was as if the marshal's greatcoat was quite forgotten.

"Marcelle!" he shouted, and moved quickly towards her.

But when he saw that she hadn't moved, and continued to present him with that solemnly austere face, he was shocked. He stopped and looked around for St Germain. But St Germain had discreetly vanished through the same side door through which he had brought the girl.

"Marcelle … " he began, rather hesitantly. "But it's truly wonderful that you are here."

She smiled a small, restrained smile, but said nothing.

"So tell me … how do you like my country?"

"Very pretty," she replied.

"What do you mean?"

"It's very pretty. Or shouldn't I have said that?"

The King swallowed briefly.

"Oh, but it is. Wonderfully so."

This was not what he had expected. He had hoped for something of the old Marcelle, some down-to-earth language of the sort he was so familiar with.

"And yet ... " he began ... "don't you find, this palace ... a bit shabby ... a twaddlesome sort of place ... in comparison to the Louvre, perhaps. Tell me it's all twaddle," he almost pleaded.

"I find it aesthetically very pleasing, and at the same time very cosy, Your Highness."

He took a step closer to her.

"Tell me, Marcelle ... or don't you remember me ... your Oscar?" His voice was little more than a whisper. "You don't remember Oscar, and how no one could have been more useless than he was, how you had to scold him all the time?"

"Of course I remember, Your Highness," she said, coldly, almost resentfully.

Her aloofness reduced him to even greater despair.

"Then why won't you talk to me as Oscar? I shall always be Oscar to you. Or are you still angry with the old Oscar, and regret the whole thing? Speak to me, the way you used to."

"Of course I'm not angry," she replied, in a strained, hesitant voice. "Of course I'm not angry with you. Oscar will always be my dear old pal."

She raised her arms towards him, but the gesture was somehow arrested half-way, and she shrunk back into herself.

"No, please don't ask me for the impossible. Your Highness is King Oliver VII of Alturia, not Oscar. Oh, Oscar was someone else entirely."

"Why? What was Oscar like?"

"Oscar was the kind of boy who could con twenty-four locomotives out of an American railroad king ... "

"I can tell you now, that story wasn't true."

"I know, Your Highness. But Oscar was the sort of boy who said that kind of thing, just to win my heart. He was a dear, dear boy."

"Please sit, Marcelle," he said, defeated. Memories flooded back, overwhelming him. His one venture into the real world ... "Tell me something about Oscar."

"I remember," she said thoughtfully, her eyes fixed somewhere above his head, "we went together once on a boat trip to Torcello. We didn't have much money so we packed some bread and ham into a bag—good fresh Italian ham and Bel Paese cheese—and we were just like the concierges in Paris going off on a Sunday to shoot at St Cloud. And on the boat they thought we were on our honeymoon. We went to the front of the boat and a wave hit us and we were completely drenched, and Oscar was afraid I'd catch a cold because the wind was up. At Torcello we settled ourselves down on the grass and unpacked our lunch, and in the bar they brought us glass after glass of wine. After dinner Oscar read *La Stampa* and fell asleep, and I tied a garland of daisies to his hat. And we were just like people on honeymoon, and those Paris concierges. That evening Oscar played his mouth organ in the lovely moonlight, and we sang. That's when Your Highness was Oscar … truly Oscar … But now … "

The King rose and paced up and down the room, deep in thought. He remembered that trip to Torcello very well. Then … he had indeed been truly Oscar then … he had been just like anyone else: like a human being …

Suddenly he came to a halt and looked at her.

"You are quite right," he said sternly, as if to himself. "That Oscar is no more. He's dead. He no longer exists. So, Oliver VII, King of Alturia, what have you to say to Mlle Marcelle Dubois, from Paris, who asks, and expects, nothing from you?

"Look, Marcelle," he continued, after a further pause. "You must at least allow me to carry out poor Oscar's last wishes."

He took the necklace from the table and held it out to her.

"Oscar sends you this gift. You remember, the poor fellow always promised that if any of his ventures ever succeeded, you would be the first person he thought of. This is poor Oscar's one gift to you."

She took the box in her hand, opened it, took the necklace out and began to fiddle with it nervously.

"Thank you very much," she said softly. "I really do thank you. It's wonderful. Miraculous. I always said that Oscar was a really good boy."

Then, with eyes full of sorrow, she added. "And I would have said the same if he hadn't sent this present to me."

She smiled, very slightly. The King came a step closer. For a moment he felt that, despite everything, something of the old passion between Oscar and Marcelle was still alive. But, with the most delicate of gestures, she stopped him in his tracks.

"Look, Your Highness, I know I have to be sensible about this. You were never really right as Oscar, and I'd probably be the same if I mixed with royalty."

For a long while the King stood there, silent and very sad. Then:

"So, Marcelle, and what will you do next, if I may be so bold as to ask?"

She lowered her gaze.

"A good friend of mine has bought himself a car and invited me to go with him to Brittany."

"That's excellent. They say Brittany is at its best at this time of year. I envy you, Marcelle. Tell me, would it be very impertinent if I asked who that person is?"

"No, of course not. Your Highness knows him well: Sandoval, the painter."

For a moment he was gripped by fierce jealousy. Oh, the lucky rascal! He always chooses the pick of everything for himself! When it comes to a profession, he paints; in politics, he's a conspirator; and now he's going off to Brittany with Marcelle, on the money I gave him as a reward for his services! But then he remembered the whole moral lesson he had brought back from his brief excursion into real life, and said, with resignation:

"Then go, Marcelle. I would have gone too, but from

188

now on my place is forever in Lara. Have a good time, Marcelle. Goodbye."

Once again she made a deep curtsey, then went out through the door by which she had entered. A moment later St Germain was back in the room.

"St Germain," the King mused, "yet again you have taught me something. If I hadn't seen her now, perhaps for the rest of my life I would have mourned for the trip to Torcello and Oscar's idyll ... But why are you putting on that face?" he asked in sudden alarm.

"Your Highness, it's a day of goodbyes and farewells. I wish to ask Your Highness' permission to take leave of you myself."

"You? Why? Where do you want to go?"

"To Buenos Aires, Your Highness. I've had a telegram from my friends there; they're expecting me. I am needed to sort out a really big business deal."

"Count, you're joking!" the King shouted angrily. "Your place is to be forever at my side. As long as I am King here, you will always have good work to do."

"I know, Your Highness," St Germain replied, with a deep bow. "I know, and I am profoundly grateful. But that is precisely why I am asking you to allow me to take my leave."

"I don't understand," the King said, exasperated. "Do you think you could find, anywhere else, a better situation than the one you have here?"

"I don't think that, Your Highness. In fact I am quite certain that some very difficult times lie ahead of me— living on the top floor of some little hotel and dining on

189

the boring menus of restaurants in the student quarter. A hundred thousand dollars is a large sum of money, but it will drift away as mysteriously as it came. And then I'll start all over again, until I am grown too old and end my worldly career in total poverty."

"So, then … ? Why would you rather not stay on as my chief financial adviser?"

"A settled bourgeois existence would never suit me, Your Highness. I'm a man for serious work. I just cannot see myself administering, writing memoranda, counting money and transacting legitimate business for the rest of my life. My financial talent is for making money from nothing and then looking for another nothing to make more money from. That's my *métier*."

"And aren't you afraid of getting tired of doing this? That the permanent insecurity might grind you down?"

"Get tired? Oh, who knows, Your Highness, perhaps I already am? But I always bear my illustrious ancestor in mind. No country's borders could contain him. New courts kept coming, and new gullible princes, new secrets and new adventures; the whole world glittered at his feet like so much treasure trove that had to be pocketed up quickly before the rightful owners came back … until he found his rest in the crypt in that little North German town … "

"But that was then, in the gorgeous pink and sky-blue eighteenth century, with its frilly lace and beauty spots. It's a bit harder to pocket things up in this modern world of reinforced concrete, St Germain!"

"Your Highness, my illustrious ancestor claimed to have

190

lived for over a thousand years, and to have known Pontius Pilate personally. And sometimes I think of myself that I too have always been here, and will live forever … Long after reinforced concrete has disappeared, the need for adventure will still be with us … But this theme has taken us rather a long way. Your Highness, give me leave to go."

"I don't know what to say. If you must go whatever the cost, I cannot restrain you by force. I can only say I shall miss you very, very much."

St Germain smiled, and bowed.

"If ever your situation changes, Your Highness, and Oscar has to be resurrected and he needs my help, St Germain will give it, even from his grave."

He bowed again, and vanished, as if he had been dropped into a magician's hat.

A few days later Princess Ortrud and her dazzling entourage arrived from Norlandia. The capital gave her an enthusiastic welcome. The whole day was given over to the celebrations. She held a reception for the female members of Alturian aristocracy, attended a banquet in the City Hall, inspected the arrangements and fittings in the so-called Queen's Wing of the palace, and only towards evening, before dressing for the celebratory night at the opera, did she find a few moments to be alone with her fiancé King Oliver.

"At last," he cried, as Baron Birker went out. He went

quickly over to Ortrud, embraced her, and gave her a gentle, intimate kiss.

"It's so good to be here," she said. "How I love this country. When I go down the street now, people shout their heads off the moment I appear. And they no longer bash Baron Birker on the nose; they write *Long live Birker, true friend of the country* on the wall of his house! Isn't that interesting?"

"It's all down to your fiancé's political wisdom," the King replied. "It turned the situation around completely."

"I always said you were a wonderful king," said Ortrud, nuzzling closer up to him.

"Tell me, Ortrud, did you miss me?"

"Very much, my dear."

They kissed again and sat down.

"And then you know," she went on, "I must confess in all honesty, when you vanished like that I was afraid I would never be your wife, and I would never know the great change they told me about that is so important in a woman's life. My mother always said how difficult it was to find a husband for a royal princess. Monarchs are getting rarer by the day."

"What? Did you think I might go off with someone else? That's not very nice of you."

"Oh no! I didn't think that; only my mother. Once you disappeared, you were impossible to trace. I don't understand how you managed to make yourself so invisible. You really must tell me where you went, when you were on the loose. What were you doing in your shirtsleeves in Kansas City?"

"I never went there. And I wasn't 'on the loose'. I was gathering experience. I mixed with all sorts of people, I got involved in stormy events, I got to know life."

"And what did it teach you?"

"Oh, so many things. Above all, that it isn't very interesting."

"What?"

"Well, that life … "

"I don't understand you."

"You don't need to. It's enough that you realise that I have learnt how good it is that there are little princesses in the world like you … in a world where there are still kings."

"Tell me, Oliver, but truly … did you miss me?"

"Of course. Very much. The fact is, I did talk to another woman … "

"What sort of woman?" Ortrud cried out in terror. "Oliver … you betrayed me all the time, I know!"

"Of course I didn't. It wasn't like that at all."

"Don't tell me, I know what men are like. Tell me, what sort of woman was she? I'm sure she was dreadful. Who did you like best?"

"Well, you see, Ortrud, in Venice there was a girl, a dear, really interesting girl. Completely different from you … "

"I can imagine what sort of girl she was. A common baroness, or a minister's wife, yes?"

"Er … er … yes, more or less. Very common, actually. That was why I liked her."

"And so?"

193

"So nothing."

Ortrud became very angry.

"Since you brought this up, you'd better give me the full story. What was this woman? Did you kiss her?"

"How could you think that? We just talked. But I didn't want to tell you. I only mentioned her because, you know, she was completely different to you, but then she also looked a great deal like you. And I turned to her, I am sure, because properly speaking, the two of us ... "

But he stopped, suddenly concerned. Princess Ortrud was really not the sort of woman you can tell everything to.

"And what about the two of us?" she asked anxiously.

Oliver dropped the earnest tone of voice he had been using and answered instead as if he were still addressing his people from the palace balcony:

"I realised I could no longer fritter my time away. I had to return to the throne as quickly as I could to marry you. Truly."

Ortrud gazed at him with suitable awe.

"You know, Oliver, it's wonderful how you foresee everything, and can plan for everything."

"To be sure."

"And that the real reason you went away was so you could return and people would really be pleased to see you."

"Yes, my girl. History teaches us that kings have to travel abroad from time to time, like husbands. Otherwise you get bored with them."

"Wonderful! And I thought it was the end of the world when you sent me back to Mama. Only, I don't understand, how when ... do you remember ... that evening ... how

194

did you know that a few seconds later the revolution would begin?"

"I could sense it. That's how it is. The soul of a statesman is like a Geiger counter."

"And what a bad time it was for a revolution. Do you remember?"

"Couldn't have been worse. You never went through that change that is so important in the life of a woman."

"And I never have since."

"But I was more than willing to help you make that change, believe me."

"Truly? … But then the sea serpent came."

"Yes, the sea serpent. The fate of Alturian kings. But then it went away again. And now it's done what it had to, and it'll never trouble us again."

"Are you sure about that, Oliver? Completely sure, that there won't be a revolution this time?"

"Quite sure. You must trust in my statesmanlike wisdom and foresight."

At that moment a terrible clamour was heard in the distance.

"What's that? Is someone shouting?" the King asked.

"Someone, you say?" Ortrud gazed at him with eyes full of reproach. "Shouting? Don't be ridiculous. It isn't 'someone', it's the mob, and they're not shouting, they're screaming. It's the sea serpent!"

They both ran to the window. Just as on that other evening, a huge crowd darkened the scene outside the palace.

"The whole country is here," the King exclaimed. "What is this?"

"Oliver!" Ortrud said petulantly. "There's going to be another revolution. Another revolution, and then ... "

"Nonsense!" the King said, with a wave of the hand, and went to the internal telephone.

"Colonel Mawiras-Tendal please."

A moment later the Colonel stood before them.

"What's going on out there?" the King asked.

"The Princess' mother, the Gracious Empress Hermina, arrived unexpectedly this evening. Dr Delorme quickly got together a little crowd to celebrate, and now they are marching to the railway station to greet her. I was just about to inform Your Highness."

Marcelle and Sandoval were walking in the hoary forest of Dinant, in whose deeps Merlin the magician lies somewhere asleep, still working his spells.

"Isn't it beautiful here?" said Sandoval.

"Very beautiful. Let's sit for a bit; I'm tired."

They sat down, and for a long time were silent. Sandoval was working on a composition in his head. "Brown", he thought, "then a little red over there ... this tree is particularly fine." Then his glance fell on Marcelle's face. It was distant, thoughtful.

"Tell me," he asked suddenly. "Do you still miss Oscar?"

"Me?" she asked, alarmed. "Yes. No. No, truly no. Because I know very well that we could never be right for each other."

"No? But you were so good together: like two lovebirds."

"Yes, that's true. But that's because somehow I always knew there was something strange about him."

"How do you mean?"

"You know, at first I thought he was a little bit stupid. But now I realise, he was always just a king."

*Coronation portrait of King Karl IV of Hungary with Queen Zita and their son,*
*Crown Prince Otto, Budapest, December 1916*

# TRANSLATOR'S AFTERWORD

Antal Szerb's last novel, written just two or three years before his appalling death in 1945, is his most thoroughly genial. The sly wit, benign good humour and capacity to surprise us at every turn are not new to his writing, but the sunniness of its view of humankind is. Devised in a world of tramping jackboots, the setting and tone have more in common with the Bohemia of *The Winter's Tale* than with Hitler's Bohemia-Moravia. Humankind may be venal, self-deceiving and self-important, and things are never quite what they seem, but there is not a harsh word in the whole book. Indeed, readers coming to it by way of Szerb's acknowledged masterpiece, *Journey by Moonlight* (1937), might be somewhat disconcerted by its apparent frivolity. Certain themes will of course be familiar, as will the subtle and pervasive irony, but gone, apparently, are the darker spiritual questionings, the confrontation with inner demons, the brooding sense of psychological determinism; and the manner is now unswervingly playful. What, such readers might wonder, has become of the writer's high seriousness?

Those, however, who arrive by way of his first novel, *The Pendragon Legend* (1934), might find it a natural development of Szerb's earlier, more nonchalant 'neo-frivolist' style, his practice of exploring real philosophical questions through the most seemingly irresponsible means. In *Pendragon* the trick was to parody different forms of popular (English) fiction, and play them off against each other to explore the instability of the self. *Oliver VII* takes this theme a step further. Licensed perhaps by his reading of Pirandello, Szerb now focuses on the connection between role-play and inner identity in a world where illusion and reality are inextricably confused. As with Pirandello, the formal artifice of the production carries the theme. Venice is treated so stagily that 'at times the whole scene seems to wobble'. Every major character hides behind some form of disguise—not least the royal hero who, oppressed by convention, plots a coup against his own throne, goes into exile, moves effortlessly into the role of confidence trickster, and ends up impersonating himself. But Szerb is no mere imitator of the Italian illusionist. Whatever casual resemblance there may be to *Henry IV,* the novel serves a very different vision of the world. What Oliver learns about the self looks not back but forward to the French existentialists, as well as insisting on less fashionable notions of responsibility and integrity.

In fact it is to the preoccupations of *Journey by Moonlight*—both overt and hidden—that *Oliver* more directly speaks. The parallels are so many and so pointed it is hard not to see the later novel, for all its lightness of tone, as a return to unfinished business. The progress of the young King sheds more than a passing light on what happens to Mihály, the protagonist of *Journey by Moonlight.* Both begin as misfits who feel stifled by convention, yearn for the 'real life' of the world 'beyond the fences' and contrive to escape by characteristically underhand means. Finding themselves in Venice, they head for its dubious underside in quest of adventure. Events force them to take stock of who they are, what they really want, and where their loyalties lie, and they are forced to choose—between two women, and whether to return to the old life. But whereas Mihály meekly submits to being fetched home 'like a truanting schoolboy', Oliver goes back for his own, distinctly honourable, reasons.

The intimate connection with the earlier novel is confirmed by a steady stream of allusions. A character lost in the 'narrow little backstreets' of Venice imagines the water swirling blackly in between them, as if 'still heaving with the forgotten corpses of past ages'—a note more appropriate to the morbidly nostalgic hero of *Journey*. More usually these echoes are given a farcical twist, as when rotund little Pritanez, the corrupt Finance Minister of Alturia, locked in a room in circumstances of comic indignity, is heard complaining from afar. The description evokes that wonderfully mysterious moment in *Journey* when Mihály is enchanted by the sound of wailing from behind a wall: 'There was a profound, tragic desolation in the song, something not quite human, from a different order of experience.' The echo in *Oliver VII* verges on self-parody.

Themes are echoed too, only to be re-examined. To take just one example: the adolescent theatricals which, in the earlier novel, shape the adult lives of all their participants like a destiny, are replaced by a set of altogether more adult games, played for different purposes and to entirely different effect. Oliver's various role-plays are entered into deliberately, with an ever-watchful eye on the consequences. Through them he acquires a fund of insight into both the world and himself and, in distinct contrast to Mihály, he comes to accept the role he has been allotted in life. For him, a man defines himself by doing what his situation requires.

In *Oliver VII*, Szerb is also seeing off demons that haunted both Mihály and his own younger self. The moral, psychological and indeed sexual confusions that *Journey* holds up for such unsparing scrutiny, in all their pathos and absurdity, had a painful resonance for their creator. Beneath the surface of the 1937 novel swarms a vigorous underlife of private reference. Mihály, haunted by the dead Tamás, the aloof, pale, fastidious young man for whom he once entertained clearly homoerotic feelings, is very much an alter ego of the writer himself. In real life, at the age of eighteen, increasingly troubled by his feelings for a schoolmate called Benno Terey, Szerb wrote a novella entitled *Who Killed Tamás Ulpius?* In it, as Csaba Nagy has shown, he attempted to exorcise once and for all the ambiguous elements in his love for the young man. The tale commits in effect a double murder, of the beloved person, now seen as a malign influence, and of the youthful Szerb himself: it is in fact a kind of joint suicide, one which finds its direct echo in *Journey*. The 1937 novel seems to suggest that Szerb, both as a Catholic and a newly married man, like Mihály, on his honeymoon, felt the need for an even deeper understanding of what happened, and perhaps a more thorough purgation. So steely is the intelligence at work that the issues are left, in the final chapter, clarified but unresolved, and the hero's ignominious return to Budapest is yet another self-betrayal, another defeat. The ending of *Oliver VII* is in direct contrast. While it too leaves us with lurking ironies and unanswered questions—every page of the novel presents a new surprise, and there are signs, for example, that Princess Ortrud may not long remain the convenient *ingénue* she has so far appeared— Oliver, unlike Mihály, does achieve a capacity for moral action to match the insight he has gained into his own divided self and divided loves, and his relationship with the now-forbidden lover ends in a scene of real dignity.

*Oliver VII*, then, far from a mere afterthought to Szerb's more 'significant' novels, is a source of new understanding of them. Indeed it is only when the three novels are taken together that the prevailing spirit of his art can be fully understood. Over the eight years his values have not so much changed as clarified, and *Oliver VII* is in some ways their most direct expression. The 'neo-frivolism' alluded to in *Pendragon* can now be seen as the subtle business it is. Szerb nowhere expands this concept into a formal philosophy—that would hardly have been in the spirit— but its implications are many and various. Its essence was caught by the religious historian Károly Kerényi, who said of the writer that "he never took himself seriously". This was more than a compliment; it exactly reflected the value Szerb attached to the 'self' as in 'self-interested' and 'self-important'. If personality is plural—as Freud, and Pirandello, knew, and *Pendragon* wittily demonstrated— then the different selves that make it up will include some very odd bedfellows. For Szerb's mentors, if that is what they were, the consequences are potentially tragic: reality is unknowable, and the poor battered ego is locked into a hopeless struggle for stability. Szerb turns that conclusion on its head. Since life, for him, is a joyous, miraculous thing, and love not entirely an illusion, the instability of the 'self' is in fact a form of release. Its inconsistent nature, and the endlessly ingenious strategies it devises to keep its end up, are necessarily comic. The art that grows from this realisation is too benign for satire, too shrewd for sentimentality; it pulls off that almost impossible trick of accommodating a disillusion bordering on cynicism with an amused, indeed delighted, acceptance of the world with all its faults. Its origins may lie as much in Szerb's religious predisposition as in any psychological theory, but the message it sends out was not a bad one for its time.

In October 1942, the questions of identity and loyalty that feature so strongly in Szerb's fiction took a new and urgent form. A lifelong Catholic and a sincere if somewhat free-thinking Christian, he found himself reclassified as a Jew (by descent) and therefore an alien in the land of his birth. Religious affiliation was no longer a defence. Now it was his turn to choose: between living out the role he had been so cruelly allotted, and the chance to flee. At first he simply clung to hope, while his scholarly works were banned, and *Oliver*, passed off as a translation from the English of a supposed A H Redcliff, sank without trace (his widow kept it in a drawer for the next twenty years). He lost the right to teach in his university; was summoned for periods of forced labour. Next came the yellow star and the ghetto. Ahead lay the death camps. He was presented with repeated opportunities to escape; someone arranged an academic post for him at Columbia University. Each time he sadly but firmly declined. Some of those close to him, such as the poet Agnes Nemes Nagy, thought he acted from naive optimism, misplaced idealism or the misguided notion that his fame as a scholar and writer gave him exemption; and those factors may have played some part. But there was also a real commitment to Hungary and to his work there ("How can I teach students who haven't read their Vörösmarty?"); and, even more, an unshakeable loyalty to those he loved. In 1944 he was officially granted permission to emigrate, but stayed because the Arrow Cross threatened reprisals against his wife. Similarly, just weeks before his horrific death in January 1945, he rejected help because his younger brother was in the same camp. On another occasion, he simply refused to leave if it meant abandoning his old colleagues and friends Gábor Halász and György Sárközy. (It made no difference. They survived not much longer than he did.) Friends wrote of the 'mood of resignation' that came over him, and the way he continued to put others first, to think of their needs when his own prospects were becoming so dark. It is impossible not to connect these attitudes with the values enshrined in his books, not least *Oliver VII*. Indeed, almost all the qualities that made Antal Szerb such a remarkable human being seem to find expression in his radiantly benign last novel.

LEN RIX

August 2007